CURATOR A

Book One in the Trilogy

To my husband, Richard, and my son, Corey, for their continued support while I wrote this book.

Chapter One
The Waterfall

Victoria Willis, or Vicky as she was known to her family and close friends, levitated in an upright position, over the river, beneath the waterfall's flow. The waterfall's almighty pressure and her exhaustion made it impossible for her to keep her head held up. Her thin body was defenceless as her arms were forced out to the sides and her legs dangled beneath her. An almost silent screech, quieter than a mouse, was all she could muster when she tried to scream.

One of nature's natural elements was no match for the invisible entity which had total control over her. The murky water relentlessly poured through her hair and over her flawless skin. She found it harder to breathe and whenever possible, she took deeper intakes of air; coughed and spluttered as she tried not to swallow the water. Her red flowery dress clung to her. Gooseflesh covered her body and her teeth chattered. Red marks appeared around her wrists. Bite marks appeared on her face and neck. Her face only became visible when clumps of her hair were pulled back and her eyes revealed her vulnerable soul.

She closed her eyes and imagined herself to be somewhere other than her own reality, until her body could take no more and she lost consciousness.

The entity let her go; it had done with her; it had had its fun. Her pale lifeless body fell into the river, and she hit the water with a thud.

*

Ben Cooper and Amanda Styles, who were Victoria's closest friends, had deserted her. The pair had screamed as they fled the scene, while the Ouija board bobbed up and down on the river. Victoria had sat beside that same board without a care in the world, with her so-called friends, a little while earlier.

*

Lisa Parkins, a timid girl, had heard laughter when she walked along the woodland path on her way home from a nature walk one late afternoon. She caught sight of the group of friends and had not wanted them to see her, so she hid a short distance away, curious to see what they were doing. She could see Beechwood Park at the other side of the river as she sat down on an old fallen tree trunk which was partially covered with green moss and hidden behind an overgrown holly bush. Once positioned, she watched them through a small gap between the branches.

The group were older than her. They had left school the year before. She remembered they had hung around school together. Ben had been her crush; hers, and half of the girls at school. In return, he had never noticed her and was not even aware of her existence. He was too engrossed with admiring his Mediterranean good looks in his reflection at every given opportunity. Amanda was his dippy on-off girlfriend.

No longer able to contain his excitement, he opened the Ouija board box. The box, which was an old brown tatty-looking object, had dust on with his fingerprints. As he reached inside the box, he treated the contents as though he oversaw the Crown jewels. He placed the board and the wooden planchette on to an already flattened patch of grass.

The friends had planned to make a day of it and had taken along a picnic, which they set up, on a blanket, beside them.

Victoria's contribution was a choice of sandwiches which she had prepared that morning. She had raided the refrigerator at home of any leftover cooked meats and salad.

Ben had remembered at the last minute and bought three packets of spicy flavoured crisps and a packet of chocolate biscuits from the corner shop on his way there.

While Amanda, who had put no thought into what to take, was more than happy with the three cans of fizzy pop she had chosen from the bargain basket in the local supermarket.

The picnic was left to one side as they sat, cross-legged, on the grass around the Ouija board and held hands.

'Is anyone there?' Ben mocked.

Victoria tittered.

Amanda and Ben laughed; tears streamed down their faces.

Victoria waited until they had calmed down. She looked at them, in turn, and put on a sophisticated voice, 'Right, you two, shall we try to communicate with real spirits now?'

He did not need to be asked twice. 'Is anyone there?' He rolled his eyes; his pupils and irises disappeared for a moment. 'Is anyone there?' Once again, he laughed at his own foolishness and then looked at Amanda to check if she followed his lead.

'Why do you have to act so stupid all the time, Ben? And why's your hand so hot and sticky?' Victoria sounded like a disgusted schoolteacher, and she had a facial expression to match.

'I don't think you want me to answer that.' His eyes twinkled. His eyebrows moved up and down, rhythmically, while he smirked and flared his nostrils. He always found the urge to wind her up too hard to resist.

'Urgh, Ben, you're a disgusting creature. Pack it in and behave yourself.' She tried to remain serious and once again succeeded; although, she almost smiled.

'Let me have a go.' Amanda let go of their hands, stretched her arms out in front of her and wiggled her fingers. She looked skywards, closed her eyes, and continued, 'You're now in my power. I'm calling out to the dark side. Is there anyone there who would like to communicate with us?'

Victoria tutted. Her patience was wafer-thin at the best of times, and she was even more irritable than usual. 'We're supposed to hold the planchette on the board for it to work, stupid people. I've seen it done like that loads of times in the movies. I'm practically an expert you know.'

'You're that all right,' he said and then waited for her to make some sort of response. He wanted to wind her up some more and he was not left disappointed.

'Go on, Ben, spit it out. I know you're dying to say something witty.'

'I wanted to say, "you're that all right".'

'What?'

'An egg spurt!'

Victoria shoved his shoulder and made him topple backwards. He rolled about on the grass with Amanda in fits of laughter. The pair squashed any daisies which had not already been flattened while Victoria shook her head and narrowed her eyes.

Lisa glanced at her watch. She could not believe how long she had been there. She got to her feet and was about to make her way home when she heard a high-pitched squeal. She was sure the noise came from someone in the group. Had they seen her? She checked. None of them looked across in her direction. She sat back down again, stayed as still and quiet as possible before she moved closer to the bush to get a better look at what had happened.

Amanda, who had got to her feet, continued to make intermittent high-pitched squealing noises as she pointed at the board. 'Look, the planchette moved by itself. It's pointing to the *Yes*.' She jumped up and down.

'Okay, calm down, Amanda. There's no need to get hysterical. The board's probably on a bit of a slope and the planchette has just slid down and, coincidentally, landed on the *Yes*. It can't move on its own.' Victoria turned to look at Ben. 'Or is this something to do with you? Are you pranking us? Come on. Own up. What have you done to it? Is the planchette magnetised or something?'

'It's not on a slant, I tell you. I saw it move. You've got to believe me,' Amanda said.

'I haven't done anything to it, I swear,' he said. 'That's the first time I've got it out of the box.'

'Where did you get the board from?' Victoria said, calmly.

'I found it in that junk shop in the village. Do you know the one I mean? The one next door to the tobacconist. The box was covered with cobwebs, and it was hidden behind some other old board games. When I asked the old man, in the shop, how much it was, he said I could take it. He never even bothered to look up from the book he was reading. He did mention it'd been in his shop for years and he wanted to get rid of it, so he let me have it, for free.' His stomach started to growl.

'Okay, let's all just chill out and have something to eat. We'll have our picnic, pack everything away and then we'll go to the pictures or go and do something else.' Victoria smiled at them to try to reassure them.

Amanda and Ben nodded simultaneously.

They left the board and the planchette on the grass to one side, sat on the picnic blanket and shared out the food. No one spoke as they ate; instead, they glanced intermittently at the board and at each other. The only noises which could be heard were from sandwiches being chewed, biscuits and crisps being crunched, and pop being slurped. The silliness and laughter had been replaced by a more sombre feel; even when he burped after he had drunk too much fizzy pop.

After they had eaten, they sat for a while. None of them wanted to leave; captivated by what they had started.

Amanda looked at Ben. 'Go on; I dare you to ask it another question,' she said.

'No way. You ask it.'

Victoria tapped her fingers on her thigh. 'I thought we were going to pack everything away once we'd finished eating and go and do something else.' She started to clear away their rubbish into an empty plastic carrier bag.

'Ben's a chicken; a big, fat chicken.' Amanda flapped her arms, up and down, and impersonated a chicken.

'What and I suppose you're not.' He no longer acted like the fool. 'Go on, prove it. I dare *you* to ask it another question.' He wanted to go home.

'Goodness me. Will you two give it up? I'll do it. We do this one more time and then we go; are we all agreed?' Victoria picked up the planchette and placed it on the centre of the board. She kept her hand on it and said, 'Who are you? What is your name? Who do you wish to communicate with?' The planchette did not move. She moved her hand away, turned to the other two and said, 'See; nothing; now let's go. This is getting boring.'

Amanda and Ben stared at the board.

Victoria rolled her eyes, tutted, and sighed, and then asked the same questions and got the same response: nothing.

They stayed still. Only their narrowed eyes moved, from side to side, when they glanced at each other.

Amanda and Ben started to laugh; Victoria joined in.

No sooner had they started when the planchette zoomed across the board and pointed to the *V*.

The laughter stopped. They stared at the board again.

The planchette did not disappoint. Seconds later it slid across the board and pointed to the *I*.

Simultaneously, Amanda and Ben turned their heads and looked at Victoria.

'What?' Victoria said.

The planchette moved again and pointed to the C.

The group were left with no doubts that the spirit wanted to communicate with Victoria.

Amanda could not take any more. She screamed, got to her feet, and ran towards her home. Ben followed close behind.

'It's okay, you two; leave me to tidy up.' Victoria did not give the spirit chance to continue to spell out her name. She got to her feet, reached down to pick up the planchette and hurled it, and the board, into the river. 'Stupid game anyway,' she shouted; hopeful Ben and Amanda might have heard.

A sudden force pushed against her chest. Winded, she stumbled backwards, and landed on her bottom. 'Ouch.' She rubbed her bottom and her chest. 'I don't know who, or what, you are or what you want with me but, please, just leave me alone.' She took a deep breath and checked around but there was nothing to see.

She got to her feet again and tried to make her way towards the towpath. But whatever was there, would not let her go. It got behind her and dragged her by her hair. She reached up and tried to stop it. The pace quickened. She lost her footings. Big clumps of her hair left a trail on the ground. Her shoes came off as she was dragged down the banking towards the river. Open sores on her legs stung and bled where she had been pulled through the tangled brambles. It continued to drag her through the water until they reached the waterfall.

'You did not allow me to finish my game, Victoria. I am here to punish you for your inappropriate behaviour and because I have waited long enough for my retribution for events long ago,' a gentle, yet masculine, voice said. It was the last voice she would ever hear, and the waterfall was where she would spend the last moments of her life while it inflicted vengeance upon her.

Ben and Amanda reached the end of the towpath. They had left behind a dust trail. Birds flapped in the treetops. Ducks squawked on the canal. They had beaten any personal best records as they continued to run in opposite directions towards their homes; neither looked over their shoulder to check on the other.

*

Ben opened the front door, left it ajar, and ran upstairs to his bedroom. He locked the door behind him and closed his curtains. He felt palpitations against his ribs. He jumped on to his bed, laid on his back, stretched his arms and legs out and tried to calm his heartbeat. Wide eyed, he stared up at the ceiling and tried to make sense of the shadows.

His mother knocked on his door. 'Are you okay, Ben?'

He jumped. 'Yes, I'm fine, Mum. I just want to be left alone.' He held up his hands, reached towards the ceiling, and tried to stop them from shaking.

His parents left him, alone, in his room and allowed him to explain what was wrong in his own time.

*

Amanda burst into the kitchen and tried to explain to her father what had happened with the Ouija board.

'Slow down, girl.' He pulled out a kitchen chair and patted the seat cushion. 'Sit down and start from the beginning.' He sat beside her and waited for her to explain.

She caught her breath; got tongue-tied; had to backtrack; eventually, she managed to explain.

'What have I said to you in the past, Amanda? Give me strength.' He rolled his eyes. 'Will you never listen? Will you never learn? I've told you numerous times to stay away from anything like that. Ouija boards are dangerous instruments. If you don't understand how something works, then don't mess around with it.' He turned his frown into a smile.

'I'm sorry, Dad. We were only having a laugh. We didn't think anything would happen.' Her tears had left mascara streaks down her cheeks.

'You said that you left Vicky by herself. We'd better go and check she's okay. Let's hope nothing bad has happened to her.' He smiled again; tried to reassure her. He tied his laces and grabbed his jacket from the hook.

She was afraid to return to where the incident had happened, but she also felt guilty because they had left Victoria alone.

On the way, he told her a story about a Ouija board and how someone he had known, when they were teenagers, had come face to face with the devil at their peril.

As usual, she appeared not to listen.

They arrived too late to save Victoria. Her body had already been discovered in the river, at the base of the waterfall where its waters still lashed down on her.

They checked the grassed area where the three of them had picnicked. Found the picnic blanket and the bag of rubbish, but there was no sign of the Ouija board, planchette or the box.

She explained to the police what had happened with the Ouija board, but they did not take her seriously.

Forensics found no DNA evidence of Victoria's attacker.

Her death certificate stated cause of death to be asphyxiation.

The police concluded that the attacker had made their move after Amanda and Ben had left the victim alone. The attacker had, more than likely, watched from nearby and waited. The victim would never have stood a chance. The police believed there were no witnesses.

*

Lisa had witnessed every detail, but still years later, she could not breathe a word to anyone about what she had seen. It was something she would have to take to her grave.

Chapter Two

Beechwood Park

Apart from the occasional peculiar incident, Beechwood Park was a peaceful place and was large enough for everyone to have their own space, if needed.

During the spring and summer months, the river flowed gently alongside the park. The waterfall could be heard a short distance away. The local wildlife enjoyed the calm. Daffodils and bluebells grew randomly, wherever they chose, to break up the dominant greens and browns. Some of the trees were full of blossom and ready for the seasons ahead. Greens, yellows, blues, and pinks were everywhere you looked, a splendour of beautiful colours.

Autumn was a magical time of year. The leaves on the trees were shades of reds, browns, and gold; too many to count. As the weeks passed, some of the trees looked vulnerable with their bare branches. On other trees, the remaining leaves tried to hold on until a gust of wind came along and defeated them, in a heartbeat, and made them fall to the ground. Lisa liked to listen to the rustling and crunching sounds as she strolled through the carpet of leaves and kicked them into the air. But the leaves quickly turned to mush, and the wind turned cold, almost overnight, and bit her deep to the bone.

The winter months were the hardest. She enjoyed the snow but could not escape to the park to play as it was too cold and sometimes inaccessible. The park lost its appeal, its vibrant colours and it became a scarier place. The river flowed deeper and quicker; became more savage and unforgiving. Never clear; more of a dirty brown colour from the stirred-up riverbed. Broken twigs, branches and leaves got dragged along its surface.

The park was her refuge when she needed space from the dramas of her everyday life, which included her family and school in equal measures. She hated school, but always attended; never played truant; even went when she felt ill.

The park was a short distance from her childhood home. She spent many hours at the park alone and often, she lost track of the time as she escaped reality into one of her daydreams. When she got upset, she had no one close to confide in or to comfort her, so she found being close to nature helped.

Her father, John, had many rules which she had to obey; one was to be home before it got dark. She never had a problem with that rule as she never wanted to hang around at the park when it was night-time anyway. There was little in the way of lighting, and the darkness attracted the wrong type of people. Families were drawn to the park during the day while gangs, up to no good, were drawn there during the hours of darkness.

She daydreamed as she swung on the old swing. Her palms had turned orange from its rusty chains. She would rinse her hands in the river before she made her way home.

It was only a couple of weeks earlier she had witnessed Victoria's murder. Even though Victoria had never been a friend, she still felt a little upset from the ordeal. When she looked across at the waterfall, the incident seemed like a distant memory. There was nothing left at the crime scene to suggest anything had ever happened.

Beechwood was a small village; word had soon got around about Victoria Willis's death. The grown-ups believed there was a maniac on the loose while the younger ones believed something far more sinister and eviller was at large. They each made up their own theories and versions of events.

In the evenings, the parents never tried to keep their teenagers indoors; instead, they made them promise to stay in groups and never wander off alone.

Most of the teenagers played in the river. Some of them dared to go nearer to the waterfall while others searched for the Ouija board amongst the brambles and further along the riverbank.

Motion sickness had set in. Lisa scraped her heels along the ground to stop the swing. To try to stop the nausea, she stared down at her legs and concentrated hard. Over the years, she had researched books about mind over matter; a subject she believed in. Confident, if she wanted something, she could make it happen, which included being in control of her body.

As she looked down, she noticed the soles on her scuffed shoes had broken free of the glue again. The patch on the knee of her jeans had started to come away at one corner and revealed the hole beneath. She picked at the stitching. The patch would need to be sewn back on, along with a new patch on the elbow of her sweatshirt.

John and her mother, Elizabeth, were always first in-line at jumble sales. Family members passed hand-me-downs on to them too. The clothes were never fashionable or the previous year's fashions either.

Without a care in the world, she leapt off the swing and ran across to the old wooden roundabout. No one else was in the park to join her, so she held on tight to the handrail, put one foot on the roundabout and hopped up and down on the ground with her other foot and made the roundabout turn. Faster and faster, she spun. She tilted her head back and closed her eyes. A gentle breeze blew across her face; made her smile. Her overgrown fringe blew upwards. She opened her eyes and looked up at the sky.

The roundabout slowed down until it came to a stop.

She felt dizzy as she jumped off and when she tried to walk in a straight line she fell to the ground. She laid on her stomach, lifted her head, and looked towards the horizon. The world appeared to have tilted and the horizon had moved to a vertical position. She squeezed her eyes shut and grasped two clumps of grass, so she did not slide off the ground into the sky.

Moments later, she dared to open one eye and then the other and exhaled a sigh of relief when everything had returned to normal.

She sat up, crossed her legs, and looked across at where the slide had once been. The council had taken it away weeks earlier because it had rusted, and patches of leaded paint had started to peel off. She had played for hours on that slide. In its place was a patch of flattened tarmac where someone had chalked a hopscotch grid.

She ran across to the igloo shaped climbing frame and clambered to the top, lowered herself through the top bars inside the frame, held on and then dangled.

She let go and dropped towards the ground. Like an Olympic gymnast, she would land perfectly and then imitate the cheering crowd. But something stopped her and grabbed her waist. She continued in slow motion, stared ahead, and held her breath. Did not dare to look at who it might be. She stopped several inches above the ground and hovered. Her body became rigid. The hands let her go. She landed on both feet.

For a moment, she did not dare to move.

She checked around the park and noted there was still no one else there. She clambered back up to the top again where she stayed seated; even when she felt the coldness of the metal through her clothes which numbed her bottom.

As she looked across at the bushes, she remembered she had been sat in that same place a couple of months earlier when she saw Victoria in there.

Victoria had looked across at her and blown her a kiss before she got frisky with her latest conquest. Quite the exhibitionist and popular with the boys, it was rumoured she had taken many boys into the bushes. Sometimes more than one at a time. An experienced young lady despite her persona of airs and graces.

Lisa's curiosity had got the better of her, so she had climbed down and tip-toed towards the bush. She had not needed to get too close to get an unobstructed view and watched Victoria and her companion for a brief time, to confirm if the rumours were true. Both were dressed in the suit's nature had provided as they rolled about in the foliage and performed strange sexual acts on each other, which Lisa had not known existed until that day.

Back to reality, she felt calm again and climbed down. Once her feet were on firm ground, she rubbed her bottom cheeks to relieve their numbness. She made her way across to where the skateboarders and BMX riders often played and chuckled to herself as she read the graffiti:

If u want sex ring; telephone number stated.

YW + BJ 4EVA TGVER 4 YRS TO CUM; a heart surrounded the initials with Cupid's arrow pierced through its centre.

Rick woz ere; month and year stated.

There was the usual oversized illustration of a penis, testicles, and sperm shaped droplets. In fact, there were several penises of assorted sizes.

She sat down on the bench beneath an old sycamore. The tree sheltered most of the skateboarding area and blocked out any sunlight. Its trunk displayed a large, engraved symbol: an upside-down pentangle. No one knew who had engraved it or why. It had been there for generations.

She looked across at the football pitch and watched two pigeons take a drink and a bath in a muddy puddle.

She had wanted to play on one of the tree swings but could not find one that was not broken. Some of the swings had been there for years and only pieces of broken rope, which dangled from out of reach branches, remained. Instead, she strolled across to the river, sat beside it and rinsed her hands.

A middle-aged couple, who were out with their dog, rushed past. They smiled, half-heartedly, at her. She did not recognise them but thought it polite to return their smile.

As she continued to watch them, she saw them stop to talk to Mrs Blake, who owned the local newsagents; a buxom lady who was nicknamed The Tabloid because she found out about most things before the local newspaper did. The three of them gossiped and, no doubt, laughed about some poor unsuspecting soul. Their chests and shoulders heaved as they threw back their heads.

A group of younger children arrived and played on the swings and roundabout while their mothers sat on a bench. Occasionally the women broke off from their chatter to watch on.

Lisa smiled when she saw the children play off-ground tig. Playfully, they shouted and pushed each other, ran around, took turns, and jumped over and on everything to escape each other.

The mothers shouted over the children's noise; told them to behave and to be careful.

The children calmed down for a short while before they continued with their noise and antics.

Lisa blocked out· the noise from the children and their mothers as she drifted into one of her daydreams.

Her favourite time of the year was summer. One of the reasons was because daylight hours were longer, so she got to spend more time at the park. She loved to lay in the warmth of the sunshine on the grassed riverbank and pretend to be someone else who was attractive, had friends and who travelled the world to the faraway places she had only seen on the television and in magazines.

Bees and butterflies flew around as she stared up at the blue sky and studied the cloud shapes. The sky had always fascinated her, a perfect blue without a cloud, or angry and stormy. She did not care which as she still found it beautiful.

A plane flew overhead and interrupted her daydream. It left behind a contrail. She looked at the cloud beside it and was convinced if she stared at it for long enough, she could make a hole appear right through the middle of it.

Beside her, a field mouse squeaked and broke her concentration. It moved closer to get a better look at her, but when she held out her hand it scurried away.

A family of ducks paddled nearby. One quacked angrily while another sounded like it laughed in response. They perched on a couple of the stepping stones which were laid across the river.

The stones were only visible when the river was low. She often used them to cross but a large gap between two of them made it tricky; care was paramount because the stones were mossy in places, which made them slippery. She had fallen in the river on a couple of occasions, which was still impressive given she had crossed them hundreds of times.

Time had passed quickly, but it always did when she went to the park. It was time to head home as Elizabeth would have dinner ready.

As she started to make tracks along the path, a gang of older boys arrived. They appeared not to notice her, as they ran past, and shouted obscenities at each other.

Andy, dark haired and lanky, made a clanging noise as he ran. The sound of breaking glass in the plastic bag he carried, followed. He hurled the bag and its contents on to the football field. It landed with the sound of more breaking glass. Vodka flowed out of the broken bottles and out of the bag.

The gang reached the furthest corner of the field and hid amongst the trees.

Adam, stocky and fair-haired, carried a fire extinguisher under his arm. He was the youngest and most naïve of the gang. Andy and Martyn had coaxed him into stealing the extinguisher from a nearby business, which he did without being noticed.

'What do I do with this syringe?' Martyn, an unfortunate looking character, who was underweight and had bad skin, said. He might as well have worn a T-shirt which announced to the world that he was a drug addict. His heroin addiction had taken its toll and had ravaged his body. He ran his tongue over the blood which trickled down his forearm from his track marks.

'Do you really want me to answer that?' Mike, whose rudeness and arrogance outweighed his good looks, said. He looked around at the others to check he had their attention. 'Is there anyone here who gives a shit what Martyn does with his syringe?'

While the rest of the gang were in fits of laughter, Martyn launched the syringe into a neighbouring field and put his paraphernalia back into his trouser pocket. High as a kite, he had not noticed the others as they mocked him.

Adam stood up, as though he were on stage. To amuse the others, he put the extinguisher's nozzle to his face and started to inhale the contents.

There were chants of encouragement from the others, 'Go, Adam; go, Adam.'

Within seconds Adam had turned white. His eyes rolled and he lost consciousness. He fell forwards but was unable to put his hands out in front of him. The grass cushioned his fall as he landed face first.

Not long after, an ambulance arrived. The paramedics did not look amused but continued to treat him without any comment. He was fortunate he had only broken his nose and had two black eyes while a visit to the dentist rectified his broken front tooth.

As the nights grew longer, the gang got noisier. They had no respect for the neighbouring homes. The residents moaned about the ongoing situation with each other.

Frank, an elderly man, had noted the gang were not locals. He had seen them get off the number twenty-seven bus at the same time every night. He reported them to the local police station, but the desk officer was not concerned with the gang's behaviour. The officer's attitude was out of sight, out of mind; the youngsters had not caused anyone any harm and had not caused any criminal damage. To skirt around the issue, Frank was asked to make a record of dates, times, and problems, which he was not happy about.

A few days later, he had got to the end of his tether and decided more drastic action needed to be taken. When he knew the lads would all be together, he walked down to the park to have a chat with them. The years had not been kind to him, and he was frail on his feet. He used a stick to help him walk.

For a short while, he observed the gang from a distance.

The gang turned their heads when they heard him approach.

Not able to work out who the ringleader was, Frank spoke to them as a group, 'Evening.' He was polite, but firm, and appeared calm.

'Evening,' Mike, the obvious spokesperson for the gang, said.

The others watched Frank but stayed quiet.

Frank looked Mike straight in the eye. 'Are you, lads, behaving yourselves tonight?' He tried to keep the conversation civil.

'Yeah.' Mike raised one side of his upper lip and gave Frank the once-over.

'What are you, lads, up to?'

'Oh, you know, a bit of this, a bit of that.'

The others laughed as they hung on Mike's every word.

Frank ignored their laughter. 'Do you think you could try to keep the noise down tonight? There's a lot of elderly residents live around here who like to go to bed early. And could you take your litter home with you?' He sighed as he felt relieved to get how he felt off his chest.

Mike turned his back on him.

'I said, do you think you could keep the noise down?' Frank paused. 'I've got a better idea. How about you all bugger off home. There must be somewhere you lads can hang around closer to home.' He was taken back to a time when he served in the Royal Navy and gave out orders.

Mike looked over his shoulder at him like he was something nasty he had trodden in. 'Do us all a favour, old man. Just *fuck off* and mind your own business.'

Frank had not served his time in a war to be spoken to in that way. He prodded Mike in the back with his stick.

Mike turned round and appeared to plume his feathers as though he were a peacock. He towered over Frank. 'What the fuck do you think you're doing, old man?'

Frank felt a little intimidated, but he did not show it and stayed calm. 'I'm asking you and your friends to keep the noise down. It's not rocket science, young man. I felt sure you'd be able to cope with a couple of simple instructions.'

Mike frowned and pointed at Frank. 'You've just assaulted me. You lay one more finger on me and I'll have you.'

Frank realised he would not get a sensible response. He raised his eyebrows and tilted his head to one side slightly. 'Do you not know what the word *respect* means?' He shook his head and then spoke louder and slower, 'Now, please, answer my question. Are you going to keep the noise down?' He paused. 'Apologies, let me ask you that again in a different way; a way you're more likely to understand. Are you going to keep the *fucking* noise down?'

Mike gaped. Then his face reddened. How dare a little, old man try to humiliate him in front of his friends? He made a fist at Frank as though he threatened to punch him.

Frank jabbed him in the stomach with his stick.

Mike stumbled backwards, lost his balance, and landed on his bottom. As he tried to get back on to his feet to have another go at him, Martyn and Andy grabbed his arms to keep him down. He did not put up any resistance but cursed under his breath.

Frank knew he was wasting his time. He shook his head again, turned round and started to make his way home.

Martyn and Andy let go of Mike.

Mike got to his feet. He told the others to stay and wait for him. He kept a short distance between himself and Frank as he followed him. He had only been gone a minute when he felt a coldness like he had never experienced before. The hairs on the back of his neck stood on end. He shuddered. Someone had followed him. Whoever was there, was close, right behind him. As he turned round to check, he expected to see one of the others and although there was no one there, he sensed something was.

That evening a police officer knocked on Frank's door. He had just put the dishes away after washing-up from his supper. Mike had followed Frank to check on his address before he reported him for harassment. The officer cautioned Frank; told him to stop bothering Mike and his friends; thought it best for everyone concerned that he stayed away from the park when they were there. He should count himself lucky he had only received a wrap on the knuckles. Charges were not brought against him.

*

It was years later when Lisa returned to Beechwood Park. She looked back on her life and realised how much she had missed the place. That visit was different, however. Not only was she older and wiser but she understood who she was and where she was meant to be. She could put the last jigsaw piece into the puzzle and move on without regret.

Chapter Three

Growing Up

Lisa grew up in a small mid-terraced house, situated on a quiet side road, off the busy road which ran through Beechwood Village.

The back garden of the house was beautiful and could have featured in a gardening magazine. Lisa and Susan were rarely allowed to play there, and Elizabeth was never allowed to hang the washing out; lines of clothes would have made John's garden look untidy. She had to take the family's wet laundry along to the launderette in her shopping trolley and use the driers there. In a funny sort of way, she enjoyed the outing because it got her out of the house, if only for a short while.

One sunny day, she was on one of her trips to the launderette while Lisa and Susan were at home in the back garden. Both were sat, cross-legged, on the lawn playing a game of snap.

John, who intended to scare them, tip-toed out through the back door. 'Get off my lawn, you stupid little girls. It's taken me years to get it in such pristine condition. Go and play somewhere else,' he shouted.

Lisa jumped. He often had that effect on her. He was a tall, well-built, man with a shaven head, dark eyes, and a square jaw, which was often covered with stubble. But he was no gentle giant.

He grinned. 'I know, I've had a brilliant idea. Why don't you go and collect registration plates from moving vehicles, preferably on the motorway?'

The family who lived next door were out in their garden and had seen his outburst.

The father, who barbequed burgers and sausages, glanced sideways at John before he shook his head and rolled his eyes.

His wife, who rested on her sun lounger, sat upright to see what the commotion was. Then she looked across at her husband before she sighed and laid back down.

Their two boys, who played in their paddling pool, stopped splashing, and frowned as they looked across at Lisa and Susan.

Before John had chance to shout again, Lisa and Susan picked up the playing cards, put them back inside the pack and stood up. With lowered heads, neither of them looked at him as they walked past, but they felt his hand smack the back of their heads.

Susan made her way upstairs to their bedroom. Lisa made her way through the house and out through the front door. She sat on the bench where he allowed them to sit if they kept to the flagged area and did not walk on any of the flowerbeds or the rockeries.

It was a pleasant warm day that day, but when it rained the puddles always appeared in the same weathered places on the flagstones. She looked at where the puddles usually formed; dried, green, circular patterns of various shades had been left behind. She listened to the sound of gentle water of the nearby stream, which flowed, out of sight, behind the trees, at the bottom of the garden.

She sat for a moment and thought about what she might do next. She got to her feet and when she peeked through the living room window, she saw John as he watched the television. She decided to keep out of his way a little longer. She made her way to the bottom of the garden, ducked underneath the branches of a tree, jumped over the stream, clambered up on to the drystone wall and walked along it. She took extra care over the wobbly stones. Once she had walked as far as she could, she turned round, made her way back, and jumped down; water splashed the back of her legs.

Rain clouds had gathered. She decided not to go to the park. Instead, she could either sit in the living room with him or go up to her bedroom. She chose the latter and decided to read. She opened the front door, closed it gently behind her and tiptoed past him so as not to disturb him.

*

She never enjoyed the colder months and wished her days away as she looked forward to the warmer months; spent most of her time trying to get warm and avoiding the rest of her family; longed for a bit of privacy, but that was impossible when she shared a bedroom with Susan.

On blustery nights, the wind whistled through the gaps beneath their bedroom window frame where the wood had rotted away over the years. The gaps were big enough that she could poke her fingers inside. To try to stop the draught, they picked out any splinters of wood before they stuck pieces of rags inside.

Early one morning, she was woken by the coldness. She got out of bed, put on plenty of layers and climbed up on to the windowsill. A thick leafed frost pattern had formed on the inside of the window panes. In turn, she pressed each fingertip and then her hand against the frost. Where the frost had melted, see-through patches were left behind. She peeked outside and noticed the frost had covered every surface.

Susan woke, sat beside her, opened her mouth wide and breathed visible vapour over the window panes to try to melt the frost.

They placed their index and middle fingers to their lips, inhaled on imaginary cigarettes, pulled them away again and pretended to exhale in a sophisticated manner.

The seamlessly never-ending season of heavy rain woke Lisa in the middle of the night as their ceiling leaked in several places: an almost nightly occurrence. The roof had leaked for years; their stained ceiling was evidence. The source of the leak was not repaired and instead the stains were covered with numerous layers of paint.

Plastic buckets had been left in one corner of their bedroom for such occasions. She positioned them beneath each of the drips. These were either emptied the following morning or before if they got full.

One such night, Lisa accidentally woke Susan.

'Are you okay?' Susan whispered.

'It's raining again.' Lisa tried to reposition her bed as quietly as she could because under no circumstances were John or Elizabeth to be disturbed.

'What time is it?' Susan tried to stifle a yawn.

'Just gone three. Go back to sleep. I've sorted everything now.' Wide awake, Lisa felt sure she would not get back to sleep.

Susan's bed was in such a position that she did not have to move when it rained. On the downside, she was next to the draughty window and at windy times, the curtains blew towards her.

Lisa got back into bed, which she had positioned in the middle of the room, closed her eyes, and tried to sleep.

'I can't sleep,' Susan said through gritted teeth. 'That dripping noise is really starting to annoy me.'

'Shush, just try.' Lisa shivered. The dripping noise annoyed her too. She also had to contend with the wet blankets from the rainwater; what's more, her blankets would still be wet when she climbed back into bed the following night. With no spare blankets or anywhere else she could sleep, she positioned herself on the edge of her mattress where it was drier. She grew weary, closed her eyes, and managed to drift off to sleep.

Because of disturbed sleep, she took on characteristics like that of a zombie as she made her way around the school's corridors. The teachers either never noticed or were not interested when she fell asleep in their lessons.

*

Lisa and Susan often squabbled about petty things which made the air feel fully charged with electricity. Lisa rarely managed to win one of said squabbles because Susan was more confident and quick-witted.

But on the rare occasions when she did win and got to watch what she wanted on the portable television, Susan would play a record to annoy her and to get the upper hand. The music would get louder and louder until it drowned out the sound of whatever she watched on the television. It depended on what moods they were both in as to whether it resulted in a physical fight or Lisa gave in and turned off the television.

Susan owned an abundance of clothes; much more than Lisa, but she complained they were mainly hand-me-downs.

They shared an old post-war chest of drawers and had two drawers each. Lisa often found some of her drawer space taken or she had to retrieve her, ripped up, clothes from underneath her bed because when John told Susan off, she would vent her frustration on Lisa's clothes.

John, who was the breadwinner, worked long hours in a warehouse. Every morning he set off to work before anyone else had got out of bed and did not arrive home until seven in the evening. Elizabeth was a housewife and she also worked, various shifts, part-time, in a restaurant kitchen, but mostly in the evenings. The couple worked hard, but they had little to show for their efforts.

Most days there was a period when their shifts overlapped, and Lisa and Susan would be left in the house alone. And without any parental guidance came sibling rivalry.

Constant reminders of how Susan was the pretty one, were of little help to Lisa's already low self-esteem. Susan was like John while Lisa looked more like Elizabeth. Not only did the sisters look nothing alike, but they also had opposite personalities.

Susan was the fortunate one in later life too. She met, fell in love, and married Karl Jones and they started a family straight away. They were blessed with two beautiful daughters, who both resembled Karl. They attended a private school; although, a different one to the one where their parents taught. Susan became a primary school teacher and Karl was the headmaster.

She was an extrovert; the adventurous one who tried out new hairstyles with daring colours and did not care what people said or thought about her.

Whereas Lisa was an introvert and not at all adventurous. She preferred to keep everything simple; then her decisions would not be judged. She cared what people thought of her, wished others liked her and had always wanted a best friend, which other people seemed to have.

One late afternoon, Susan had swigged from a whisky bottle as she laid on her back at the top of the garden. In-between swigs, she sang merrily; songs, like the ones they sang in morning assembly when they were at junior school. She had gone to a friend's house after high school, and they had got themselves into a stupor. Easily led, she would have done anything to keep in with the in-crowd. She had gone home to continue drinking by herself. Besides the whisky, she reeked of cigarettes.

Lisa had found her and persuaded her to go into the house and up to their bedroom. She poured what was left of the whisky down the drain and threw the bottle into next door's dustbin.

Susan was sat on the edge of her bed when Lisa entered the room.

'I'm going to have to tell Dad when he gets home from work; you know that don't you?' Lisa always found it necessary to try to take on a maternal role in their parents' absence. 'It's for your own good. He'll probably be able to smell you as soon as he comes through the front door anyway.'

'Tell him. I don't give a shit,' Susan slurred. 'I'll tell him what you get up to in his greenhouse; what you've done with lots and lots of boys in his greenhouse.'

'What! What are you talking about?' Lisa frowned. 'You're drunk. Stop making up lies. I'm only trying to look out for you.'

'I'm not drunk.' Susan's face was expressionless; although, it appeared she found it difficult to focus. 'I can handle my alcohol, thank you very much.' She paused. 'And I'm not lying either. It's you that's the liar.' She paused, again. 'Anyway, shut up. Why do you think you can always tell me what I can and can't do? You're not my mother.'

'Because you shouldn't be drinking, but I'm guessing you already know that don't you?' Lisa had to admit she was impressed by Susan's ability to still string a sentence together, albeit slow and slurred. Susan was obviously used to the drink. But what she was even better at was turning an argument around to make it seem like the other person was in the wrong. Lisa wanted to help her, so she ignored the childish comments and continued, 'Where did you get the alcohol from and where did you get the money from to pay for it? And why're you drinking alone? If something's wrong, you can always talk to me you know.'

Susan's head had started to spin. 'Listen to you. What's with all the questions, Little Miss Perfect? *You* shouldn't be kissing boys in Dad's greenhouse.'

'Oh, shut up, you stupid girl!' Lisa said. 'I'm trying to help you, but the only thing you seem interested in is self-destruction. Well, go ahead; drink yourself to death; see if I care.'

Susan, who got bad-tempered, even when sober, launched herself at Lisa. She threw several punches to various parts of Lisa's body and despite her drunkenness, aimed accurately.

Lisa managed to defend herself up until that last brutal punch where Susan pulled back Lisa's hair which forced her head back and then Susan punched her between the eyes. Lisa saw stars circling above her, like the illustrations in a comic strip.

Susan let go of Lisa's hair.

Lisa lost her balance and stumbled backwards. She landed on her back on the floor and managed to catch her breath before Susan went for her again. Dazed, but ready, she raised both legs above her and with all her strength pushed Susan up into the air.

In, what appeared to be, slow motion, Susan crashed down on to the floor. The walls and floor shook.

Out of the corner of her eye, Lisa saw an orb of light fly through the bedroom door. She turned her head and caught sight of it before it vanished into the table.

On said table, where the television and record player were, was an old jam jar with several pens and pencils inside. They started to spin around the rim while the jar remained still.

Susan turned her head and looked across at the jar.

They got to their feet. Both still shook from the adrenaline rush. Susan stood bolt upright while Lisa walked backwards and lowered herself until she was sat on the edge of her bed.

The pens and pencils continued to spin.

When Susan approached the jar to get a closer look, she was pushed from behind. It was not a hard push, but it was enough that she overbalanced. She fell forward on to the broken television antenna and nicked her neck. 'Ouch.' She put her index and middle fingers up to her neck to check for blood. Her neck smarted but it was only a surface scratch. She spun round to confront Lisa but noticed she was still sat on the edge of her bed.

Wide-eyed, Lisa gaped and stared at her.

Neither said another word.

Susan got out a cardboard box, which she had decorated with flowery wrapping paper, from behind her headboard and looked inside at her record collection. Lisa picked up her magazine, laid on her stomach on her bed and flicked through its pages; although, she did not read its content.

A short time later, once the arguments had stopped and the ambience had returned to normal, the pens and pencils stopped spinning; it was as though nothing had happened.

Lisa found an air-freshener aerosol under the kitchen sink and sprayed it around the house.

Susan rubbed toothpaste over her gums and ate a teaspoonful to try to mask her alcohol breath. Surprisingly, she did not vomit, but she missed dinner and went straight to sleep.

They decided not to mention anything to their parents about the alcohol, argument or what had happened afterwards. When they asked Lisa about her black eyes, she said she had got into a fight at school.

A few days later, they had another squabble. Not much tension had built-up, and no punches had been exchanged, when John's leather belt, which hung by its buckle on a hook behind their bedroom door, started to swing. The belt had been put there to remind them if they misbehaved, he could easily retrieve it and lash them with it. Neither of them had touched the belt nor had anyone been near the door to make it happen. The belt struck the doorframe with a regular tempo, left and right, while its buckle stayed on the hook.

When without warning, the belt stopped and remained still.

*

Other unexplained incidents occurred when the adults were not home: ornaments often flew horizontally from the mantel piece, travelled with speed through the air up to a certain distance, and then fell to the floor; however, there were never any breakages.

They witnessed ghostly figures: a young girl, dressed in Victorian period clothing, wandered around the house, more often seen as she descended the stairs; an elderly man, who sat in John's chair beside the fireplace, would lean forward and pick at shrapnel wounds on his legs; whistled wartime tunes were often heard from some unseen source.

They never mentioned any of the events to anyone else as they thought they were normal and other people experienced the same things.

*

The living room was the nicest room in the house; not perfect, but the only room which looked like someone had tried to decorate. The furniture was not too bad in there either. It felt comfortable and was the only warm room in the winter because it had a fire. The downside was Lisa had to sit with the rest of her family in that room if she wanted to keep warm.

The décor in their bedroom was in a poor state of repair: wallpaper and paint peeled off. She would pick at the loose bits beside her bed when she got bored and then mask the walls with posters of pop stars from her magazines.

Her mattress was worn, uncomfortable and the springs poked in-between her ribs. No matter what time of year it was, her bed always had too many covers on, which made it feel like there was a heavy weight on top of her. In the warmer months, she took some of the covers off, folded them, and placed them underneath her bed, but Elizabeth always put them back on the next day.

The partition wall between Lisa and Susan's bedroom and their parent's bedroom was thin. Every night Lisa had to listen to Elizabeth's moans and John's grunts as her parents had routine sex. The same noises greeted her when she woke most mornings. To try to block out the noises, she pressed her ear against one end of her pillow and wrapped the other end around the back of her head to cover her other ear. However, it did not always work or drown out some of the other noises; like her parent's headboard as it banged against the wall and echoed like a kettledrum, or their bellies as they slapped together.

Even though there was a couple of years between Lisa and Susan, they were always made to go to bed at the same time every night. Bedtimes were always early, and it made no difference if it was a school night or not. Most nights Lisa was never tired, and she laid for hours, hidden underneath her blankets from the lurking shadows.

When she got home from school, she would always be hungry and check the kitchen cupboards and refrigerator, even though she knew they would be empty.

Elizabeth went to the corner shop, daily, to buy what was needed for dinner; not always a filling meal as the portions were small, but the food was always wholesome. She did the best she could with the pittance she earned.

Lisa suffered from arachnophobia, and she found it almost impossible to use their outside toilet. Everyone else she knew had a toilet in their bathroom. More spiders found refuge in the outhouse during the colder months, and not only did she have to tolerate them, but the toilet seat would also be frozen. It was always the same routine: check for any eight-legged critters, pull down her knickers, brace herself, count to three and sit down as she gasped for breath. The door never closed properly either; she had to put one leg out in front of her, so as not to be interrupted, and check she did not pee down her leg at the same time. If no one else was about she would pee behind the outhouse instead. Soft toilet paper was non-existent at their house; instead, there were squares of soggy newspaper fastened together on a piece of knotted string.

Some nights, while she laid in bed, she would need the toilet, but would try to hold on until morning as she did not like to get out of bed when it was dark outside; sensed something stared at her through the opening of the bedroom door. She never dared to check; instead, she pretended to sleep while everyone else in the house slept peacefully.

Elizabeth was a thin, pale lady who looked like she was afraid of her own shadow. Her greasy hair always looked in need of a trim. She wore oversized glasses which looked too big for her face and did not rest properly on her nose.

To try to keep Lisa and Susan under control, when they fought, she often said, 'wait 'til your father gets home. He'll sort the pair of you out.' They spent the next few hours worried if she would say anything to him because they feared what his punishment might be. But she rarely told him because she preferred a calm home and the fear itself was punishment enough.

After a busy day, she would prepare dinner for the family before she went out to work a shift.

One evening, John had slammed through the front door, after an obvious hard day at work, and flopped into his chair.

No sooner had he sat down when Elizabeth appeared from the kitchen with his meal on a tray and placed it on his lap. 'How was your day at work, John?' She overlooked his lack of manners, smiled at him, and leant forward to kiss him.

He turned his head away. 'What a stupid question. How do you think my day was?'

She no longer wanted to continue with the conversation as she knew where his temper would lead. She moved away from him and got ready for work; bit into her bottom lip as she tied her laces.

Lisa and Susan had already eaten and were upstairs, in their bedroom, doing their homework.

'Are you trying to kill me, you stupid woman?' He sprung to his feet with the plate in one hand. The tray fell to the floor. 'This food's not cooked properly!'

There was nothing wrong with the food. He had just wanted to vent his frustration.

She ducked before his plate flew over her head. The plate smashed against the wall. Bits of food slid down towards the floor. She sighed as she would need to clean up the mess which would make her late for work.

He punched her in her eye, leant over her and then shook his fist in her face. 'Don't sigh at me again or you'll get another blackeye to match that one,' he said through clenched teeth.

Years of experience had taught her not to answer him back. She gave no clue as to what she thought as her facial expression remained blank. But she was clearly shaken as she got up from the floor, went into the kitchen and got a damp cloth. She wiped the food off the wall and picked up bits of food and the broken plate from the carpet. She would clean-up properly when she got back from work.

Before she put on her jacket, she dashed upstairs, tried to cover her reddened eye with concealer and put on a pair of sunglasses.

Lisa and Susan had heard his outburst. They knew the best option was to stay in their room and not to make a sound.

He appeared calmer as he sat back down and switched on the television.

Elizabeth walked behind him on her way out through the front door and closed it gently behind her.

*

Every Saturday afternoon John made his family sit down to watch the television together. The programme would either be a sporting event, the news, or a wildlife documentary.

If any of them made a sound, he told them to shut up and turned up the volume. They were also made to sit still. 'Children should be seen and not heard,' he said.

If a cleavage or breasts appeared on the screen, Lisa cringed with embarrassment because she knew what would follow. 'Wow, look at the tits on her. I wish your mother had a pair like that,' he would say to no one in particular. It always made her feel saddened for Elizabeth.

Elizabeth never looked at him; instead, she feigned a smile as she looked at her girls and shrugged. She hid her pain and put on a brave face for their sake but cried later when she was alone.

No one ever dared to stand up to him.

*

Their family holidays were never anything to write home about. They always stayed in the same grotty flat in Cleethorpes; never went away in the summertime and were possibly the palest children in their school.

He got up early each morning to go to the local newsagents for his paper and forty cigarettes; woke everyone else in the flat as he thudded around. Most days, he had smoked them all before dinner, so he went out to buy more.

Elizabeth stayed behind and waited for Lisa and Susan to get up. Once they were up, they got washed, dressed, and sat at the table while Elizabeth prepared a full English.

He always took his time at the newsagents. It was only a two-minute walk to the nearest one. She never asked what took him so long though.

When he returned, he sat in an armchair and opened his newspaper. He glanced at the headlines and paid particular attention to the naked girl on page three. When he had finished, he folded it in half and placed it on the coffee table.

Like clockwork, he picked up the television remote control and put on the news. He never spoke to anyone until he had finished his morning routine.

Once everyone had eaten, Elizabeth washed-up and cleared away.

Most of the morning, they sat around the flat and either waited for the rain to stop, or to see what he had planned for the rest of the morning. If they went out, the whole family had to get back so he could have a lunchtime nap. Elizabeth, Lisa, and Susan tiptoed around the flat so as not to waken him. He never allowed Elizabeth to go out alone or with Lisa and Susan. After lunch, and his nap, they either walked along the seafront or through the park.

Lisa was envious of other children in her class; some travelled abroad for their holiday, and some went more than once a year. They went on aeroplanes and came back with glowing tans. One girl in her class always seemed to have an all-year-round tan. Lisa had never even seen an aeroplane up close, let alone stepped inside one.

Overall, she thought her childhood was a disappointment and she had missed out on a lot of fun. She never got asked to birthday parties but watched as invitations were handed out; listened to their excited chatter, before and after. When she had wished them a happy birthday, they smiled and said, 'thank you.'

*

Christmas was her favourite time of year. An exciting time when the family got together. She only saw some of them at Christmas because they lived a distance away.

Elizabeth's parents had lived in Spain for years. Grandad Buckley wanted to live somewhere warm because he suffered with arthritis and the warmer climate made his aches and pains more bearable. Grandma Buckley wanted to live wherever her husband wanted to be. She would have followed him to the moon. But Christmas was always spent in their hometown. They were generous, affectionate grandparents who gave Lisa and Susan lots of kisses and cuddles.

John's birthplace was Cornwall, where his parents still lived. He met Elizabeth when she holidayed there with her parents. They always tried to convey it was love at first sight, but everyone knew they had to get married because she was pregnant.

Grandma and Grandad Parkins were not quite as generous and were much stricter; nearly regimental. They had plenty of money; however, they did not like to spend it. A Christmas get-together appeared to be more like a chore to them with their countless sighs and their long faces.

Grandad Parkins never complained about Elizabeth's cooking though, which he managed to devour every year.

'Waste of bloody money,' he often said. 'A load of commercialised rubbish. Most of these young ones, today, don't even know what Christmas is really about.'

One year, he made Lisa and Susan cry when he told them Santa had committed suicide because he was fed up with the government and the state of the country. John found it hysterical. Elizabeth, on the other hand, found the joke neither funny nor proper. It took her a while to convince the girls their grandad had lied.

Once everyone had arrived in the morning, the whole family sat in a circle and exchanged gifts. In the background Christmas tunes played on the radio while everyone squeezed and rattled their gifts before they opened them. Lisa and Susan always received more than anyone else.

Grandad Buckley helped put the new toys and gadgets together while Grandma Buckley tidied away the gift wrap, tags, and ribbons.

Grandma and Grandad Parkins neither offered nor tried to help; instead, they sat and waited for lunch to be served.

All the grown-ups started early on the spirits as they chatted and caught-up with everything which had happened. Even John appeared happy. The sound of laughter filled the air. Elizabeth hurried around the kitchen as she prepared lunch; a little too merry on the free-flowing wine.

When it snowed it was magical, even if it was just a flurry. The only day of the year when Lisa did not want the sun to shine.

The fire was ablaze as they sat around the table for Christmas lunch. No one ever ate the dates or twiglets which were put out to nibble on. They never had a starter; if they had, they might not have had room for dessert. Lunch was always the same impressive feast: turkey, sage and onion stuffing, Yorkshire puddings, seasonal vegetables, and gravy. Every year, John carried the turkey through from the kitchen; it was his job to carve it.

Lisa often thought how funny it would be if he tripped and landed face-first on the table as he carried the turkey through.

And no matter how much she ate, the food on her plate never seemed to lessen.

Dessert was always Christmas pudding; the adults had brandy sauce and the children could choose between custard and ice cream. When everyone had finished, Elizabeth brought out coffee with cheese and biscuits.

Lisa would titter when Grandad Parkins always fell asleep straight after lunch.

'You could set your watch by him,' John said. He was convinced Grandad pretended to be asleep, so he did not have to help with the washing-up.

After lunch, once everything was washed-up and cleared away, everyone settled down to watch the Queen's speech and then a movie.

But Christmas Days would pass quickly, and Lisa always felt sad when the family left.

On Lisa's birthdays, Elizabeth baked her a cake, handmade her a card and placed a small amount of money inside. She always bought a magazine and chocolates.

Every one of those cards were still tucked away in a shoebox in the bottom of her wardrobe.

In the run-up to Easter, Lisa and Susan received chocolate eggs from all their close relatives. But they were never allowed to eat chocolate during Lent and always had to save their eggs until Easter Sunday. The eggs were displayed on top of a Welsh dresser and it tormented Lisa to look at them every day. When the day finally arrived, she ate chocolate until she felt sick.

Easter Sunday, Christmas Day and birthdays were the only days when they were allowed to indulge in anything sweet, like chocolate.

*

Punishment came often and was usually severe. There was never any room for second chances in their house, which was why Lisa spent most of her childhood scared of John.

One such punishment happened one Sunday morning when she had woken early and switched on the television. She had been following a series called Around the World in Eighty Days by Phileas Fogg and Passepartout. She changed the channel, laid back in bed and waited for the programme to start. The volume was low, so as not to disturb anyone, but, somehow, John still heard.

'Get in this *bloody* room now, Lisa.' His voice bellowed around the house. He did not seem to care that he had woken Elizabeth and Susan.

Susan's snoring stopped. She opened her puffy eyes and furrowed her brow as she looked across at Lisa.

Lisa got out of bed, turned off the television and made her way towards her parent's bedroom with her head lowered.

'Get in that corner, face the wall and put your hands on your head,' he said as she entered. 'Do not speak or move until I tell you. Am I making myself clear?'

'Yes, Dad,' she said. Even though she was tired of all the punishments and upset she had missed that episode, there was no trace of an attitude in her tone as she did not want to aggravate him further.

She had been stood for some time. Her legs started to ache. Pins and needles set in, but if she dared to move without his permission a worse punishment would follow.

With his head rested against a pile of pillows, he laid under his covers and chain-smoked. The ashtray on his bedside cabinet overflowed with cigarette butts. Sprinkled ash was on the cover, down the side of the bed and on the floor. The room was smog filled because with little ventilation, a tiny gap beneath the window was not enough for that amount of smoke to escape quick enough.

Elizabeth laid beside him, like an obedient servant who did not dare to speak out against her master.

Lisa found it increasingly harder to control herself. She tried not to cough; wanted to rub her reddened eyes; tried not to overbalance and touch the nicotine coated wall.

He sat up, placed his cigarette in the ashtray and reached behind him for a pillow. He aimed it at Lisa and threw it. The pillow struck the back of her head, made her lose her balance and hit her face against the wall. 'Right, you've had plenty of time to think about what you've done wrong. In future, young lady, if you wake up early on a Sunday morning, you lay in bed until I tell you that you can get up. You *do not* turn the television on and disturb the rest of the house. Am I making myself clear?'

She turned round to look at him. 'Yes, Dad.' Her eyes welled up, but she did not cry.

'Go on.' He gestured for her to leave. 'Get out of my sight.'

She did not want him to see her tears and kept her head down as she ran out.

Susan was still in bed with the covers tucked up beneath her chin. Through tired, teary eyes, she watched Lisa as she got back into bed and saw the large, red bump above her eyebrow.

As Lisa rubbed her arms and legs, to soothe the pins and needles sensation, she smiled at Susan.

Susan turned over and closed her eyes.

John picked up his cigarette to take a drag. 'Aargh, bloody hell!' He leapt out of bed. Somehow the cigarette had turned round in the ashtray, and he had put the lit end to his lips.

Neither Susan nor Lisa dared to move.

Elizabeth leapt out of bed and ran downstairs to get butter from the refrigerator to put on his blisters.

*

Lisa was fifteen years old when she had to avoid the communal showers after a games lesson.

'Grab a towel and get yourself into the shower, Lisa,' Miss Aitken, a short, stocky teacher with a crew cut, who always stood at the end of the shower block as though getting into the showers was a life-or-death situation, said.

Lisa did not look at Miss Aitken as she answered, 'Sorry, miss. I can't today. I'm on my period.' She surveyed the towels, which were the size of handtowels and only covered your modesty at best.

Miss Aitken's chubby index finger, with badly bitten nail, moved down the list of names on her register. 'But you were on your period last week, Lisa.'

'My periods are irregular, miss. They're all over the place. I'm sorry, miss. I can't help it.' Lisa, along with several other girls, used that same excuse because she knew Miss Aitken nor any of the other teachers would have ever asked her to prove it.

Miss Aitken tilted her head slightly to one side, narrowed her eyes and looked at her. 'Okay, Lisa. I'll mark your reason down on the register.'

The truth was, Lisa was a late developer and had not started her periods. The real reason was because she had not wanted anyone to see her bruises. Her bottom and lower back were black and blue; although, the bruises had started to fade. She had changed into her games kit in one of the toilet cubicles, so the other girls did not see. She thought it easier to cover up the truth than be forced to explain to others while they pointed at her and judged.

Two weeks earlier, a minor incident had happened at home and neither Lisa nor Susan could admit to it. An empty milk bottle had been broken on the front doorstep. It never seemed to cross John's mind that the bottle could have been knocked over by an animal. He never gave them an opportunity to discuss it either.

'Come over here, *now*, Lisa.' He had decided it was his fatherly duty to hit Lisa and Susan, in turn, until one of them owned up to the incident.

As she made her way towards him, she tried to reason with him, 'Please, no, Dad. It wasn't me; I swear.'

'Pull your knickers down and bend over my knee.' He had a glint in his eye, as though his words gave him some sort of perverse pleasure. He reached out, grabbed her by the wrist, and pulled up her skirt; ripped her knickers as he yanked them down. He took off his slipper, bent her over his knee, struck her bottom several times and then pushed her off. She landed, on her knees, on the floor. Her knickers were wrapped around her ankles as she got to her feet. Tears rolled down her face.

As John struck Susan, she flinched and looked across at Lisa; tried to convey, through her eyes, that she needed help.

After several more turns of the slipper, the pain became too excruciating, and it was obvious Susan would not give in. 'I did it,' Lisa said without another thought. 'I'm sorry, Dad. It was an accident. I didn't mean to do it.'

'At last, you've had the courage to own up.' He threw the slipper to one side and started to hit her with his palm: a slap for every word, 'Never. Tell. Me. Another. Lie. Again. Or. You. Will. Get. Smacked. Twice. As. Hard. Next. Time.' There was a short pause where she prayed, he had finished. 'Do. You. Understand?'

Her skin stung as though it was alight. 'Yes, Dad,' she said as she continued to lay across his knee. A panic came over her. She needed to pee and was not sure how long she could hold it in, and she did not dare ask if she could go to the toilet. Too late; she was wet; worse still, so was he. She started to cry.

He pushed her off his knee again.

She put her hands out to break her fall.

'You, dirty little bitch. You've pissed down me.' He looked down at his trousers and screwed up his face. 'And why the hell are you crying? Shut up or I'll give you something to cry about.' He gestured for her to leave. 'Get out of my sight before I do something I'll regret.'

She pulled up what was left of her knickers and ran out of the room before he had chance to say anything else. She felt so unhappy, she wanted to die.

Susan followed.

They stood in their bedroom, looked at each other and then hugged and cried.

*

Lisa had always tried to make John proud of her, but nothing she ever did was good enough. She realised she was on to a losing battle when she overheard him and Elizabeth, one night, when she was halfway down the stairs as she went to get a glass of water.

'Please don't be like that, John,' Elizabeth said.

'If *she* hadn't come along, I could've been a doctor. That girl ruined any chance of me having a career. We could've been living a much better life than this one.'

'I know the pregnancy was unplanned, but we can't turn back the clock. We have to make the most of what we've got. I'm happy; why can't you be?' She sounded like she might burst into tears.

'We should've listened to my parents. You should've had an abortion. They practically begged us.' His voice quivered.

Lisa could not listen any more. She tiptoed back up to her room, got back into bed, curled up on her side and wept quietly, so as not to waken Susan.

*

At school, Susan never let Lisa hang around with her and her friends. Neither did she stick up for her when she got bullied on the school bus.

The situation got so bad Lisa avoided looking at her own reflection, be it in a mirror, a shop window or anything else.

She started to walk to and from school alone; no longer caught the school bus, even if the weather was bad, and crossed over the road to avoid any gangs.

The last time she caught the bus, other pupils name-called and chanted, and she did not know who some of them were.

'Freaky, Lisa,' one of the bullies said.

Some were right behind her, their breath in her hair.

'Lisa smells yeasty,' another bully said.

While another chanted, 'Oxfam reject, Lisa.'

They continued to torment her and behaved like a pack of wolves while other pupils, who had not name-called, sat back and laughed.

The two main culprits were not gifted in the looks department either: the boy was lanky and had goofy teeth; the girl had bright ginger, wiry hair. However, the pair were part of the in-crowd because their parents had money and could afford to buy them nice clothes.

Lisa looked ahead and pretended the bullying was not happening to her. She never let them see how much they hurt her.

Her bus stop approached. She had planned to run off the bus, but when she stood up, she was too tense, and her knees would not bend properly.

The abuse continued after she got off. An eraser flew out of the bus's back window and bounced off the back of her head.

The bullies had not hurt her physically, but she was an emotional wreck. With no one to turn to, she headed for the park until she could face going home.

A few days later, karma intervened for the two main culprits. The pair decided to do a suicide pact. They waited until his parents had gone out and made their way into the garage. She got into the front passenger seat of his dad's car. He attached a pipe to the exhaust, poked the other end through a slightly opened window in the back of the car and then he got into the driver's seat. He turned the key in the ignition. As the car filled with exhaust fumes, they held hands and died.

*

Worrall Valley High School had been a nightmare for Lisa and some of her memories from there would haunt her for the rest of her life.

She walked around the school alone during breaktimes and lunchtimes as she tried to hide away from others.

She never looked forward to the games lessons as she thought it unfair when the teacher looked for volunteers to pick their own teams.

'Four volunteers needed to pick teams for a rounders competition,' Miss Aitken said.

Lisa put up her hand, but the popular, confident girls always pushed their way to the front and put their hands up as high as they could.

'Me, miss,' a pretty, tall girl with long black silky-looking hair said.

'Oh, please, pick me, miss,' yet another pretty, tall girl said.

They were chosen, along with two of the other popular girls.

Miss Aitken never noticed Lisa's hand in the air.

Lisa was unsure if she should feel angered because she had been ignored, again, or if she should retch because of the popular girls' grovelling behaviour.

The four chosen girls behaved like they were on the stage of a Miss World beauty pageant as they stood at the front and turned to face the other girls. They started to pick their best friends, the girls who were good at games and then the stragglers. Lisa was always one of the last to be picked.

She made the reserve bench on the netball team; enjoyed hockey, even after a vicious game where she got bruised shins and her ankles swelled up; tried her best when she played rounders and always finished in the top twenty when they went on a cross-country run.

*

She gave up any hope that John could be proud of her after Parents' Evening in her final year at high school. She received a glowing report from her teachers: a bright student; although, needed to build up her confidence and join in with class discussions.

The walk home from school after said Parents' Evening was quiet and tense, more so than usual. She looked up at him, smiled and waited for him to congratulate her.

'What is it with you, Lisa?' He frowned.

Her smile faded and her facial expression became vacant. What did he mean?

'You can't do anything right, can you?' He rolled his eyes and shook his head.

She was lost for words. What had she done wrong?

He grabbed her shoulder, stopped her from walking any further, leant over her and ran his facial stubble down her cheek.

She winced as a tear ran down over her sore skin. Still confused as they continued to make their way home, she remained quiet.

Not a word of praise was received from Elizabeth either.

*

Lisa had worked hard at school every day and tried her best at everything. She was ambitious: wanted the big house, nice car, and exotic holidays. She wanted everything she never had as a child. She had always dreamt of a place at university to study to become a doctor, but by the time she was sixteen she gave up on that dream. Instead, she sat her exams, left school, and took the first job that came along.

She left home and ventured out on her own. She was more than ready to take on the world outside.

Chapter Four

The Recipe Book

Lisa moved in with a work colleague. Michelle Shaw, who got on with her parents, had wanted her own place for a while but could not afford to live alone. The colleagues had not known each other for long but anything had to be better than living at home.

They did not have to pay a deposit or a bond. The landlord allowed them to decorate the house as they wanted. The house was small and had enough outside space, at the back, for a dustbin and a length of washing line. It had a proper bathroom with an indoor toilet.

Lisa had her own bedroom, which was small but at least she could shut the world out whenever she needed privacy. Michelle had the larger of the two bedrooms. They had flipped a coin to decide who got which bedroom before they moved in.

They split the bills fifty-fifty and bought their own food; sometimes they shared. They drew up a rota for the housework.

They got on well and the more Lisa got to know Michelle, the more she liked her.

Michelle appeared to be a lot older than the two years which was between them. Everyone noticed her when she walked into a room. She lit up a room with her good looks and bubbly personality.

She made the decision to have a housewarming party the first Saturday night they moved in. Everyone, who was invited, had to take either a bottle of wine or a pack of lagers. Most of the guests were her friends; crazy people who knew how to party.

The experience was new to Lisa, and she loved it. She had only ever had a couple of sips of lager in the past, so it was not long until she felt tipsy. To make up for lost time, and with a little persuasion, she tried her first joint. After which, she appeared to develop super hearing, followed by a splitting headache and nausea. She took a couple of painkillers.

A police van drove up and down the road; no coincidence: one of the neighbours had rung them to complain.

The partygoers were one-step ahead, though. They had lookouts who signalled when the police were in sight. The music got turned down, the lights were switched off and the partygoers outside knew to hide. It reminded Lisa of a children's party game: musical statues.

The party ended in the early hours of Sunday morning. Everyone, who was still at the party, stayed overnight. The floors were covered with restless bodies. Some tried to sleep on the staircase. A couple squeezed into the bathtub. All night, bodies clambered over each other to use the toilet, find more alcohol and drugs or to find somewhere to vomit. No one slept.

Daybreak arrived. The inside of the house looked like a tornado had swept through. One partygoer stirred, and then another; until they had all risen. Everyone looked like an extra from a zombie film. They collected their belongings and started to leave. No one offered to help clear-up the mess.

Lisa's head pounded. She took another couple of painkillers and drank a glass of cola.

The smells in the house were a combination of cannabis, alcohol, vomit, and farts. Lisa and Michelle opened all the windows, wide. For hygiene reasons, they wrapped tea-towels around their noses and mouths and knotted them behind their heads.

How many people had there been at the party? There was an unbelievable number of empty bottles and cans. They gave up counting after they had filled the first two bin bags.

Lisa had not minded clearing-up the empties, but she retched a few times when she had to clean-up the vomit and the used condoms.

It took them most of the afternoon to clean-up. When they had finished, the house smelt more like a hospital with the overpowering smell of bleach.

Over the following weeks, Lisa started to relax and came out of her shell. She made new friends at her packing job at S.T.A. Sports (Beechwood) Ltd. They stocked anything to do with the sporting world. Not her dream job, but she enjoyed it, earnt her own money, had her freedom and no one judged her or breathed down her neck.

She looked forward to the future. The loneliness of her childhood became a distant memory. She made up for her sheltered upbringing: worked hard and played hard.

Michelle snuck her into nightclubs on Friday and Saturday nights; diverted the bouncers' attention with her big green eyes and noticeable cleavage and flirted with them outrageously. Her technique never failed. It went on week after week. They would get home at around three in the morning; never saw what was left of Saturday and Sunday mornings; rose from their beds in the afternoon; left on their pyjamas as they recovered and then went back to work on Monday morning.

One night, Lisa was woken by voices which sounded to come from the bathroom. She turned her head to check her alarm clock. The time read a little after midnight. She laid still and questioned herself. Was she mistaken? Had the voices come from people who walked past, outside?

Michelle continued to snore, rhythmically, in her room.

Lisa started to doze.

The voices started again: slow, deep, and calm.

She tried to listen to what the two men said, but only caught part of their conversation.

'The girl who lays awake, her name is Lisa. She is not to be touched and is to be left alone at all costs,' the first man said.

'Yes, I understand.' It went quiet for a moment. 'What about her friend; the one who sleeps?' the second man said.

'Michelle is Lisa's friend. She must also be left alone.'

The hairs on the back of Lisa's neck stood on end. She sat up and considered for a moment if she knew or should know them, but she did not recognise either of their voices.

How did he know their names? How had they got in? What were they going to do? Were they burglars? But Lisa and Michelle did not have many possessions or anything of value to steal.

Lisa was too afraid to challenge them alone.

The voices stopped. She waited a moment before she got out of bed, put on her slippers and dressing gown, and tiptoed towards her door. The door creaked as she opened it. She popped her head out through the doorway. Michelle was still sound asleep.

The bathroom door was ajar. Were the men still in there? The street light outside the front of the house lit the landing. She tiptoed towards the bathroom but found the room was empty.

As she crept downstairs to check, she kept a careful watch. But there was no one there and nowhere for the two men to hide. All the windows and doors were locked.

Her eyes widened. She started to perspire. Were they in Michelle's room? The only room in the house she had not checked. Her heart pounded like a drum as she made her way back up the stairs. She stopped at the top, held on to the handrail and put her hand over her mouth to try to stifle the sound of her heavy breathing.

Michelle had stopped snoring.

Lisa tiptoed towards Michelle's door, pulled down the handle and opened it slowly. Michelle was curled up on her side, asleep. Lisa sighed with relief when she discovered the men were not in there either. She closed the door, made her way back to her room, and got into bed. She tossed and turned the rest of the night and heard Michelle as she got up the next morning.

Michelle sounded to be in a good mood as she hummed a made-up tune while she showered.

Lisa decided not to mention the voices.

Later that day, they decided to take it in turns to have the run of the house, so they could invite guests over and make them dinner. The other one would either stay in their room or go out. Lisa thought the idea sounded fun. Several times, she invited John, Elizabeth, and Susan, but there was always an excuse. In the end she gave up.

She had bought a recipe book – Common-sense Cookery for Wally's – a couple of weeks earlier from a bookstore in the indoor market. She loved to experiment and spice up the recipes. Michelle borrowed the book and did the same for her guests.

The arrangement appeared to run smoothly. They worked hard, went out to clubs, and Michelle invited friends and family over to eat; however, one night, without warning, Michelle appeared edgy.

Lisa was sure she had not said or done anything to upset her. She checked the rota. It was her turn to vacuum. She picked up empty bottles from the floor and tidied first.

'Every time I turn round, you're there, getting in my way. Get out of my face! Why don't you go out with your friends or go and see your family? Just leave me alone,' Michelle said as she squinted through her frown.

'I'm sorry, Michelle.' Lisa could not think of anything else to say; after all, Michelle was the one who always invited her along, wherever she went.

Michelle grabbed a small glass vase from the centre of the mantelpiece. 'Aargh, you freak.' She threw it at Lisa.

With quick reactions, Lisa ducked. She was surprised the vase missed her. There was no smashing sound either as the vase appeared not to hit anything. She looked up, cautiously, and will never forget the look on Michelle's face.

'What the … It just vanished.' Michelle gaped.

Still slightly shaken from Michelle's outburst, Lisa did not answer. She thought it best to leave the room and as she made her way up to her room, she heard Michelle repeat herself.

'The vase vanished into thin air.' Michelle's facial expression was still one of disbelief.

Things started to go back to normal after a few days; however, Lisa was still wary of Michelle and kept out of her way, initially.

Michelle apologised, repeatedly; said she had no idea why she said what she did.

Lisa never spoke about Michelle's outburst or the vase incident, which was never seen again.

At work, they no longer spent breaktimes or lunchtimes together, which felt strange to Lisa to start with. However, she soon got used to her own company again.

At weekends, Michelle went out to clubs with her friends while Lisa made her excuses and stayed in.

During which time, Lisa did some serious thinking and decided she needed to make changes in her life. There were plenty of things she wanted out of life. She started to make a list: first, she wanted to learn to drive and buy a car; second, she wanted to own her own home. She would never amount to anything if she continued to spend all her money on drinking and clubs. She needed to save, but her building society savings book showed the grand total of ten pounds. She had a lot of work to do.

Michelle continued with the club scene. When she got home in the early hours, she did so quietly, so as not to waken Lisa. In return, Lisa got up quietly on Saturday and Sunday mornings. The arrangement worked well, and Michelle was always there for Lisa if she needed someone to talk to and vice versa.

Weeks went by. Michelle got to a point where she did not go out much either. The club scene appeared to be behind them. Instead, they watched a film together or Michelle read in her room while Lisa was in her room. The ambience in the house was quieter than when they had first moved in.

One evening, while Michelle had visited family, Lisa relaxed at home in her room. She felt peckish and decided to make a cheese and ham sandwich – her favourite filling – with a bit of pickle. She started to make her way towards the kitchen, but only got as far as the top of the stairs when she was greeted by a black shadow. The human shaped apparition was so big it filled the top of the stairs. There was no way she could get past it, and she would not try to walk through it.

It kept still as though it wanted her to see and question what it was.

Although, she felt no fear, she could not move. The only sound was her deep breathing. It was not an illusion, and she would not wake from a dream. Should she know what or who it was?

It faded away.

She stayed still for a moment. Part of her wanted it to reappear as she wanted to know what it was, why it wanted her to see it and what it wanted with her.

No longer hungry, she turned round and went back to her room.

Michelle arrived home with one of her cousins. Both wore sunglasses; even though it was dark outside. As she opened the front door, they fell through the doorway in hysterics.

Lisa wondered what the commotion was. She made her way down the stairs.

Michelle looked up the staircase and smiled. 'This is Siobhan, my cousin.' She poked her finger into Siobhan's cheek. 'She's got a bit of a gob on her, but she's harmless enough once you get to know her.'

'Hi, Siobhan,' Lisa said.

'Michelle, make me and Lisa a cup of tea, will you?' Siobhan flopped down into the chair. 'There's a good girl.'

'What did your last slave die of? Make your own tea, you lazy moo.' Michelle tittered.

'Go on, love. We need a cuppa, don't we, Lisa?' Siobhan looked at Lisa and winked. 'You want a cuppa, don't you? Tell this lazy mare will you.'

'I'll have a drink please, if you're making one, Michelle.' Lisa's politeness sounded out of place.

Siobhan sniggered. 'Where did you find this one?' She followed Michelle into the kitchen.

Lisa felt herself blush. She sat down, waited for her drink, and listened to them as they giggled. They sounded like little girls who had been allowed to stay up past their bedtime.

Siobhan walked back into the room with Lisa's drink. Michelle followed close behind. Siobhan handed a cup of tea to Lisa and held the cup part so Lisa could get hold of the handle. 'There you go, Lisa. Get that down your neck.'

'Thank you.' Lisa smiled and thought maybe she should not judge people on her first impression.

Michelle and Siobhan sat either side of her. They watched her as she drank her tea and did not take their eyes off her until she had finished every drop. They sat back, continued to chat about random things and giggled.

A moment of silence followed.

Siobhan studied Lisa's face. 'Hasn't worked,' she said.

'Give it time.' It was obvious Michelle knew what Siobhan talked about. 'You said it doesn't work the same on everyone.'

Siobhan slowly waved her hand in front of Lisa's face.

Lisa pulled her head back and frowned. 'What are you two talking about?'

'What do you see when I do this?' Siobhan continued to wave.

'You, waving your hand in front of my face.' Lisa was ready for the next complicated question. Michelle took off her sunglasses and put them down beside her. Her pupils were dilated. Siobhan took off her sunglasses. Her eyes looked the same; although, one of her eyes appeared to be bigger than the other. Lisa had never seen her before so was not sure if that was what she normally looked like and she thought it rude to ask. Her gut instinct warned her to be suspicious. 'You two are up to something. Have you put something in my drink?'

'What does it matter?' Siobhan's shoulders slumped. 'It hasn't worked anyway.'

'It was an LSD tab.' Michelle smiled as a way of an apology.

Lisa, who felt violated, yet calm, did not respond. She was mesmerized by Michelle and Siobhan's appearances. The cousins had turned into animals. Lisa tilted her head to one side and examined them closer. Siobhan resembled a pig with her upturned nose; a big fat sow who wore an untidy blonde peroxide wig. Michelle resembled a cute little monkey with big eyes.

Lisa waved her hand in front of her own face and experienced illusory palinopsia. She got to her feet and wiggled her arms. 'Wow, I feel amazing.' She raised her arms above her head and pirouetted.

Michelle looked at Siobhan. 'It's worked.'

Siobhan reached into her handbag and pulled out a compact disc which had a compilation of dance music tunes on. She rushed across to the player and put the disc in. The music started. Like an excited schoolgirl, she rushed into the kitchen, towards the sink and squirted washing-up liquid into the bowl.

Michelle and Lisa followed.

Siobhan turned on the hot water tap and swished her hand inside the bowl.

Michelle and Lisa watched.

'You've got to watch the bubbles; they're amazing. Look at all the vibrant colours,' Siobhan said. 'Like millions of sparkling precious gems.'

Michelle and Lisa stood either side of her and looked down into the bowl. In a trance-like state, they all hallucinated.

Lisa's cheek started to itch but the harder and faster she scratched, the more intense the itch became.

Michelle heard the scratching. She turned her head to check where the noise came from. She reached across and pulled Lisa's hand away from her face before she scratched down to the bone.

Lisa had already torn through her skin; however, the cut would not leave a permanent scar. She looked down at her nails. There was blood beneath the tips and over her hand. She started to panic.

'Don't worry.' Michelle grabbed Lisa's shoulders, looked her in the eye and tried to console her, 'It's not as bad as you think. We'll get you cleaned-up and then we'll all go out for a walk.' With her fingertips, she brushed Lisa's hair away from her face. 'Okay?'

Lisa took a deep breath. 'Okay.' She sighed.

Michelle cleaned Lisa's hands and face and administered first-aid.

They went out for a walk and stopped beside a field.

'Follow me.' Siobhan led the way with a hop, a skip, and a jump.

Michelle and Lisa followed.

The three of them laid in the middle of the field, with their arms stretched out to the sides, and looked up at the stars.

'Holy shit.' Lisa no longer felt the discomfort from her cheek. 'I'm flying.' She laughed.

Siobhan and Michelle looked across at each other and laughed.

With no idea of what the time was or how long they had been out, they made their way home.

They were thirsty when they got back. Siobhan got a carton of orange juice from the refrigerator, got three glasses from the cupboard, and poured each of them a drink. 'Drink this, you two.' She handed them a glass each. 'Packed with vitamin C which will help lower your high quicker.'

'What?' Lisa frowned. She had no idea what Siobhan meant as she was not familiar with druggy terminology.

'Yes, it can be quite a bumpy road,' Siobhan said.

'It's my first time too.' Michelle put her arm around Lisa's shoulders. 'We'll be all right together.'

Lisa needed the toilet. She pushed Michelle away and rushed upstairs. She did not have time to close the bathroom door behind her but did manage to pull her knickers down in time.

For some strange reason, Siobhan had followed her. She got as far as the top of the stairs when she was greeted by the black shadow.

Lisa could see the black shadow from where she was seated.

Siobhan gaped. 'What the? Michelle, come and have a look at this. Tell me if you can see it as well,' she shouted down the stairs.

The black shadow rushed forward as she turned back round. It passed through her and made her lose her balance. She fell backwards and bounced to the bottom of the stairs.

The black shadow was gone.

'Did you see it?' She laid at the bottom of the stairs with an obvious dislocated shoulder.

'See what? Siobhan, look at the state of your shoulder!' Michelle pointed. 'We need to get you to hospital.' She helped her get back on to her feet.

Siobhan lowered herself on to the bottom stair and cradled her lifeless arm.

Lisa flushed the toilet, washed her hands, and made her way down the stairs. She stopped halfway.

'I'm telling you; it was a big black mass and it passed right through me.' Siobhan turned her head to look at Lisa. 'You must have seen it; did you?'

Lisa sat down on a stair. 'See what? I didn't see anything. Maybe you've had one of those bad trips you told us about, in more ways than one.' She laughed.

'Not funny, Lisa! Whatever it was, it scared me half to death.' Siobhan scowled. 'My shoulder hurts.'

'I'll ring for a taxi and get them to take you to A&E.' Lisa no longer felt intimidated by Siobhan's behaviour. 'You'll be all right going on your own, won't you? Michelle and I have work tomorrow. God knows what state we'll be in. We can't afford to lose our jobs.'

'No, don't worry about me, I'll be fine,' Siobhan said sarcastically.

Michelle, who had already left the hallway, was curled up into a ball, on her side, on the living room carpet, with a cover over her head. Lisa called for a taxi before she laid near her and put another cover over her own head.

The taxi arrived a few minutes later. The driver knocked on the door. Siobhan left.

Both had forgotten to set an alarm and it was gone ten the next morning when they were woken by a fire engine as it sped up the road with its sirens blaring out.

Michelle, who looked a little worse for wear, sat-up and massaged her lower back. 'Took me ages to get off to sleep.'

'Me too. My brain wouldn't shut down. Worse still, we're late for work. Look at the time.' Lisa got to her feet. Every part of her body ached. 'That light, shining through the window, is killing my retinas. I can feel them burning.' She put her hand over her eyes to shield them.

Michelle stood up, made her way towards the front door, and opened it. As she squinted and shielded her eyes from the light, she wondered why everyone who walked past stared at her. She turned her head to look at Lisa and whispered, 'Why the hell's everyone staring at me?'

Lisa shrugged. 'I don't know. Maybe it's because you look like crap.' She laughed, half-heartedly, as she tried to make light of an awkward situation and she hoped Michelle might have smiled.

Michelle locked the door and then closed the blind and curtains in the living room. She made her way across to the telephone and rang work. 'Good morning. Could you pass a message on to the lady who works in Human Resources, please?' A pause. 'Thank you. Could you let her know Michelle Shaw and Lisa Parkins won't be in work today? We've been up half the night; think it's something we ate last night.' Another pause. 'Yes, I'll call again tomorrow if we haven't improved.' As she put the handset back down on to the cradle her shoulders drooped. 'I'll see you in a few hours.' She crawled upstairs, went to her room, and collapsed on her bed. Within seconds she was asleep.

Lisa followed her upstairs. Her sleep was deep and undisturbed; the best she could remember.

Later in the afternoon, she was woken by the smell of cooked bacon and eggs as it drifted underneath her bedroom door. She decided she would have a soak in the bath before she went downstairs to join Michelle.

Make-up free and with her wet hair tied up, she burst into the kitchen and greeted Michelle, 'Good afternoon and how are you on this fine day?'

'Good, thanks. How are you?' Michelle looked one hundred percent better than she had earlier. She put her arms around Lisa and hugged her.

'I feel good and surprisingly refreshed. Don't know if it was the sleep or the bath; probably both.'

'There's bacon keeping warm under the grill if you fancy a sandwich?' Michelle reached up to get a plate from the cupboard before Lisa had even had chance to answer.

'Yes, please, that'd be nice. I've woken up starving.'

'I forgot to mention with all the excitement and goings-on yesterday.' Michelle raised an eyebrow and smiled. 'I bumped into an old boyfriend on my way to Siobhan's yesterday.'

'Did you?' Lisa said. 'By the way, have you heard from Siobhan? Do we know if she got to the hospital okay?'

'Oh, she'll be all right. She's a tough cookie. I'm sure she'll ring me later.' She paused. 'Anyway, listen, his name's Danny.'

'Okay, go on, tell me more.' Lisa bit into her sandwich.

'He's still cute.' Michelle's eyes twinkled. 'He was with one of his friends who's cute too.'

'Is one bloke not enough for you?' Lisa winked.

'Funny, ha-ha. His friend's called Jason. I've invited them both round for dinner tonight.' Michelle waited for Lisa to object.

'Okay, I'll make sure I don't cramp your style. Don't worry, I'll get out of your way.' Lisa winked again.

'What're you talking about? Jason's coming round to see you. I've fixed you up. I promise you're going to love him. We're going to have a double date.'

'Oh, I'm not sure.' Lisa had butterflies in the pit of her stomach. 'I don't think I like the idea of going on a date with someone I've never met.'

'Oh, come on, please. You haven't got any other plans, have you?' Michelle got increasingly excited as she tried to convince her, 'Don't be nervous. Honestly, you'll be fine. Listen, they're both in their late twenties, have their own cars and have good jobs. I told him about you and he's keen to meet you.'

'Okay, I suppose it can't hurt.' Lisa knew she would not get any peace until she agreed. 'It's only dinner, after all, isn't it? What time?'

Michelle raised her eyebrows. 'About seven?'

They washed up their plates, tidied them away and then Lisa made her way upstairs to decide what to wear.

Most of the contents of her wardrobe were piled on her bed. In the end, she chose a pair of black skinny-fit jeans and a plain white T-shirt; concluded Jason could take her as he found her.

Michelle had long since chosen her outfit: a silky green dress. She prepared dinner: spicy meatballs with pasta; followed by lemon meringue pie. Both recipes were from Lisa's recipe book; the best four pounds and ninety-nine pence she had ever spent.

Lisa cleaned downstairs. She did not want to let Michelle down and wanted to make a good first impression.

At seven, Danny and Jason arrived with a loud knock on the door.

Michelle had not wanted to appear too keen. She answered the door after they had knocked for a second time and invited them in. Lisa chuckled at her behaviour.

She thought Michelle would have kept the better-looking one for herself; although, they were both good-looking and well-groomed.

The evening went well with plenty of laughter as they chatted over dinner. Danny and Jason asked lots of questions. They wanted to know more about what Lisa and Michelle did and talked about their own work. Questions bounced round about favourite food and what music everyone liked to listen to. There were no awkward silences. Everyone thought dinner was delicious and complimented the chef.

Not long after they had eaten, Michelle dragged Danny up to her room; not that he put up any resistance. The noises which emanated from her room left little to the imagination.

Lisa felt awkward and thought it a good idea to preoccupy herself. 'I'll clear the table and do the washing-up. You're more than welcome to help if you like.'

Jason got to his feet, put his arm around her shoulders and tried to pull her towards the stairs. 'Leave them; the dishes can wait. Come here!' His ego was about to take a tumble.

She wriggled from his grasp. 'No!' Her response was forthright. She continued to clear the table and with a plate in each hand, headed towards the kitchen.

'Why not?' He frowned, tilted his head to one side, and then followed her.

'Because I don't want to.' She put the plates on the worktop. 'I don't even know you. We've only just met.' She turned round to go back towards the table.

He stood in front of her, put his hands on her shoulders and looked her in the eye. 'Yes, you do! I told you plenty about myself over dinner.' He smiled; thought it might help his cause if he turned on the charm.

'No, thank you,' she said, adamantly, as she continued to look him in the eye.

He took his hands from her shoulders. His smile turned into a snarl. 'Prick tease!'

Astonished by his reaction, she watched him as he put on his jacket and tied his laces. She was confused: a man she had only known a couple of hours had expected her to sleep with him on their first date. She was still a virgin and wanted to save herself until that special someone came along.

The front door slammed behind him.

As she cleared the table and washed-up, she tried to put the incident to the back of her mind. She sang along to the tunes on the radio to drown out the upstairs noises and debated with herself if she should go out or stay in.

She turned on the television and sat down.

The hallway door opened. A flushed Michelle and Danny appeared. He pulled up the zip on his trousers while she grinned. 'Where's Jason?' she said as she scanned the room.

'Don't know.' Lisa shrugged, aimed the remote at the television and turned down the volume. 'He left a while ago.'

'Oh no! Didn't it work out?' Michelle gaped.

'Would appear that way. I don't think I was his type.' She feigned a disappointed facial expression.

Danny, who was already near the front door, put on his jacket and tied his laces. 'Thanks for a lovely evening, ladies. I'd better go find him.'

'Ring me,' Michelle said, as the front door slammed behind him.

'Are you okay? I'm sure he'll ring.'

Michelle's feigned smile showed her lack of confidence.

She was quiet for the next few days until Danny telephoned and then her mood changed instantly. 'We're going to the cinema on Friday. Come along, if you want, Lisa.'

Surprised by the invitation, Lisa smiled and raised an eyebrow. 'Thanks for the invite but I'll have to decline; two's company, three's a crowd and all that.'

Michelle and Danny started to go steady. Lisa was happy for her; plus, she got the house to herself more.

Michelle told Lisa what Jason had told Danny about her: he had wasted his time with her; she was not his type anyway, and he did not want to see her again. Lisa was not saddened by the news.

She had taken the day off work to catch up with household chores and to tackle a pile of laundry, when, unexpectedly, Danny called round. She was home alone, so she answered the door. 'Hi, Danny. Sorry, Michelle's not in. She's at work all day.' She was sure he knew Michelle would not be there.

'That's okay, Lisa. It's you I've come to see. I needed to see you while Michelle wasn't here.'

'Oh, what for?' She could sense an air of tension and tried to lighten the mood. 'Sounds serious! Are you planning a surprise and need my expert advice?'

He stared at her.

'You'd better come in.' She made her way towards the kitchen. 'Can I get you a drink?'

He followed her.

'How did you know I wasn't in work today?'

'Michelle mentioned something the other day.' An uncomfortable silence followed before he said, 'You do know it's you I want, don't you?'

She gasped. 'Pardon! Can you repeat that? I think I must have misheard you.'

'You're the one I've got feelings for, not Michelle. I had to carry on seeing her so I could get closer to you.' He appeared satisfied his behaviour was acceptable.

'I'm sorry, Danny. You're making me feel uncomfortable. Do you know how wrong what you're saying sounds? I'm going to have to ask you to leave. Let's pretend none of this happened. I won't mention anything to Michelle.'

'Don't be scared, Lisa.' He moved closer and put his arm around her waist. 'I know you want me too. I've seen the way you look at me.'

She gasped. 'What the hell's wrong with you?' She tried to push him away, but he was a lot stronger than her. 'I can assure you I've got no feelings whatsoever for you. You've got it all wrong. I don't know where you've got that idea from. It's all in your head.'

He started to kiss her neck and face.

She shuddered.

He put his hand up her top and fondled her breast.

Her eyes widened. For a split second, she froze. 'Get off me!' Why couldn't she scream? She wished someone would appear to help. She managed to push him away and stepped back.

But he stepped forward. His facial expression made it known he would not take no for an answer.

Without a thought, she reached out to the side of her and felt for the closest item she could find: the recipe book. She grabbed it, swung her arm round, and hit him as hard as she could on the side of his head.

He lost his balance and stumbled but managed to regain his balance. To say he was furious was an understatement. 'You, little bitch!' But when he reached forward to grab her, he stood upright and then froze, like a soldier on military parade. A vacant facial expression replaced his angry one. His complexion was ashen and dark circles had formed around his glazed over eyes. The transformation happened within seconds.

She watched him as he turned round and made his way towards the door.

Five small black shadows appeared and hovered beside his feet. They did not cast a shadow as any definite object would. Each appeared to have a life of its own.

He left and closed the door behind him.

All felt calm again.

She sat, for what felt like an eternity, in shock. What had stopped him? Should she tell Michelle? But what would Lisa say? Would Michelle believe her? Should Lisa contact the police? What if he had already been to the police? After all, she had assaulted him.

A few hours passed by. Michelle did not arrive home at her usual time. Lisa bit into her bottom lip and tapped her fingertips on her thigh. Had he got to Michelle first and lied? Was she too angry to go home? Why had the police not been? Lisa felt sure he had planned to attack her or, worse, rape her. How would she explain what had happened to the police and to Michelle? She had no evidence. It was her word against his.

She decided to keep herself busy and got on with the housework but was not able to concentrate on one job for long before she moved on to another.

Keys rattled in the door. The door opened. Michelle walked in. She had cried lots; her eyes were red and puffy.

Lisa looked across at her. She had gone over in her head, repeatedly, how she would explain to her what had happened with Danny, but when she saw her, her mind went blank.

Michelle looked across at her with a blank facial expression. 'He's dead!'

'Did you say dead? Who's dead, Michelle?'

'My Danny. He's dead.'

'What! How the hell can he be dead?' Part of Lisa felt relieved. The other part felt saddened for Michelle.

'He was found up by the reservoir in his car. Looks like he committed suicide,' Michelle blubbered. 'I can't believe it.'

Lisa was confused and lost for words.

'I thought he was the one. I love him so much, Lisa. We talked about moving in together, getting married and having children. I wanted two but he wanted more.'

Lisa moved closer to her, put her arm around her and rubbed her shoulder.

'I must have driven him to it. He never said anything was wrong. We were *so* happy.' Michelle looked her in the eye. 'What would make him want to take his own life?'

Still lost for words, Lisa's head spun. Inside, her chest felt heavy, and her heart throbbed. Should she tell Michelle what had happened? But what would that achieve? She sat with Michelle as she cried some more.

The next morning, Lisa packed an overnight bag and went to stay at Valley View Bed and Breakfast. She needed time alone to make sense of what had happened.

To ensure Michelle coped, and so she was on hand if she needed anything, Michelle's mother stayed with her.

*

Daniel Wood, or Danny as he was known to his friends, had walked out of Lisa's house and made his way towards his car: a well-maintained green MG convertible. All men had to have something which was their pride and joy to feel complete or so Lisa's father had told her. Not in the right mindset to drive, he got into the driver's seat and sat for a moment, in a hypnotic state.

He turned the key in the ignition and drove about a mile. His facial expression never changed. He pulled up on a narrow lane which ran alongside the reservoir. Reputed to be a bit of a lothario, he was familiar with the area as he had visited it numerous times with many girls. Of course, Michelle refused to see or believe any of the hearsay and always insisted he was not like that when he was with her.

He opened his door, got out, made his way towards the back of the car, and opened the boot lid. The side compartments inside the boot, where he kept his gun and illegal substances, were not obvious. It later transpired not all his monies were from legitimate earnings. He half-heartedly checked to see if anyone was around, took the loaded gun out and slammed the boot lid shut.

He sat back in the driver's seat, opened his mouth slightly, and placed the muzzle between his teeth. Without a second thought, he pulled the trigger. His brains formed a symmetrical pattern on the rear window.

An old lady, who had walked her Yorkshire Terrier, found his car with him inside. His blood splattered car sent her dog into a frenzy. The dog had run round in a circle and yapped. She stood beside the car and shouted for help. Her feeble cries were heard and answered by a young man who was out jogging.

The police traced Michelle from Danny's mobile and contacted her. She was the last person who had spoken to him.

*

A couple of days later, Michelle's mother went home, and Lisa returned from Valley View Bed and Breakfast.

Michelle was quiet in the lead up to his funeral. She never went out of the house and told anyone who wanted to visit that she was too busy. She looked exhausted and made no effort with anything.

Lisa got over her initial guilt after she deduced, she had never encouraged him, had not pulled the trigger, or made any suggestion he should have done so.

He had a good attendance to his closed-casket funeral. An allegiance of female admirers snivelled into their tissues. Several people were in denial that he had passed away as they never got to see him to say goodbye.

Lisa saw Jason at the funeral. He made no effort to speak to either her or Michelle.

Lisa and Michelle went out to a club a couple more times, but Michelle was never the same. There would be a part of her which was gone forever. She blamed herself for his death and could not get over what had happened. But if Lisa had told her the truth about what had happened on that fateful day, it would not have helped. It was another secret she would have to take to her grave.

Michelle and her parents decided it was in Michelle's best interest if she moved back home with them. A few weeks later, she was diagnosed with clinical depression, referred to a therapist and put on medication.

Lisa, who did not want to move back in with her parents, continued to live alone in the house and managed to make ends meet financially.

She visited her parents occasionally and because she did not live with them, she felt she got on with them better. However, if she started to visit too often, John thought it was an open invitation for him to belittle her and would judge her appearance or a personality flaw. Even though, he hurt her feelings, she never reciprocated with her own insults because she did not enjoy confrontation and it was doubtful that he would have been able to take the criticism.

She continued to work at the factory and saw Michelle occasionally. Michelle took a lot of time off due to her illness. Her doctor struggled to balance her medications. She had lost her bubbly personality and no longer lit-up a room when she entered.

A couple of years passed. Lisa decided it was time to leave the factory when she was offered a call-centre job. She said goodbye to Michelle, but it felt like she spoke with a stranger. They lost touch after Lisa left. She had a lot to thank Michelle for. Michelle had taught her how to be herself and not allow others to intimidate her.

Chapter Five

Love and Marriage

At first, Lisa spent most of her time alone at her new job at the double-glazing company. At break times she went out for a walk or read a book in the canteen. Her colleagues hung round in little cliques which made her feel like an outsider. They were friendly but there was not much time to make friends when she had her ear pressed against a handset as she tried to talk to potential customers all day.

Every day was the same. She arrived at the open plan office to a partitioned off desk which had a thick print-out of names and telephone numbers to work through, a script to read from and keep to, a pen, a pad, and a telephone atop of it.

Several months had passed when one Monday morning, a group of new starters arrived. Every first Monday of the month a dozen new enthusiastic individuals appeared; however, the majority would not see the week out.

Promoted to telesales leader, one of Lisa's responsibilities was to show the newbies what to do and go through a script with them. If they wanted to succeed, they needed to be tough and not sensitive as most potential customers were rude, would swear and then slam the telephone down. She advised them on techniques on how to try to stick to their scripts while they remained calm. No matter how tempted they were, they must never be rude back; that was the hardest part of the job.

One newbie stood out. Her eyes were drawn to him as he walked through the doorway. She felt her face redden as she realised, he had seen her stare, but she could not stop herself, no matter how much she tried to look away.

He smiled, bit into his bottom lip, and looked down at the floor. A second later, he made his way towards her and held out his hand to introduce himself, 'Hi, I'm Steven.' He smelt irresistible as he towered over her.

She noticed his large masculine hands as she held out her hand. 'Hi, I'm Lisa.' She still felt flushed; tried to scrunch up her toes; found it did not help.

She rounded up the newbies and escorted them into the conference room. The downlights came on as they entered. The tables were in a u-shaped seating arrangement, so no one could hide at the back of the class. The room smelt musty. She opened a couple of windows while everyone chose a seat. The chatter and laughter quietened.

She stood at the front, faced everyone, and introduced herself. As usual, she had butterflies in the pit of her stomach. As she explained what the company was about and what was expected of each of them, her attention kept reverting to Steven's dark eyes.

As an icebreaker exercise, each of them had to tell the others a bit more about themselves. She was more attentive when it was Steven's turn.

'Hi, everyone. I'm Steven Brook.' He paused, put his hand up and scanned everyone in the room. 'I've never worked in telesales before, so this is a whole new experience for me. I've tried other lines of work before, but none of them were for me. I hope I'm on the right track now and look forward to a career in sales.'

She sighed; he had not divulged any personal details. She started to hand out the scripts, stopped behind him, leant forward and inhaled the scent of his musky aftershave. She imagined but resisted the temptation to run her fingers through his dark hair. She had never felt that way about anyone before.

He blushed.

The other newbies appeared not to have noticed their teacher had a crush on one of her pupils as they concentrated on the other introductions.

The training session went well. The new team appeared keen and ready to start. Time would tell if a couple of the smart alecs would survive. Every session always had at least one; someone who thought it was their job to make the rest of the team laugh.

The rest of the day went fast. She was tired and ready to go home when Steven approached her. 'There's a few of us going out for drinks on Friday, after work, if you fancy it, Lisa. Nothing posh. Just the local. We thought it'd be a good way to end the week and get to know each other better.'

She was pleased to have been invited but did not want to appear keen and said, 'Sounds good; although, I've got plans later that night so I can only stay out for a couple.'

'Friday it is, then.' He smiled and raised his eyebrows.

After work, she walked home with a spring in her step; although, she kicked herself when she looked in the bathroom mirror that evening. 'I've got plans later that night.' She scowled. 'What plans? Who're you trying to kid? What's wrong with you? Get a grip. He's gorgeous. Don't you dare scare him away.'

As the week dragged on, each day saw less newbies until Steven was the only one left.

He leant against her partition and looked over at her. 'Wow, that was a hard week. I'm drained.' His eyes twinkled.

'You're not kidding.' She put the End of Week Progress Report, which she had just finished, on to her desk and turned round. 'Well done for seeing the week through. You've managed to get some good leads for the sales team. Good bit of commission coming your way if they manage to do their bit.' She paused. 'Do you think you'll be back in on Monday?' She hoped the answer would be yes.

'Yes, sure will. I quite enjoyed it, once I got over the initial rejection part from the customers that is. And I learnt a few new swear words along the way.' He laughed. 'Anyway, are you still up for a drink or do you need to get off to your other plans?'

'Mine's a lager and black. I'll grab my bag.' She reached under her desk.

The Wagon and Horses was about a hundred yards along the road from work. A quiet pub. The paintwork and wallpaper were coated with nicotine. The carpet was covered with cigarette burns. An old man propped up the bar and chatted with the landlady who looked like she might have been part of the original fixtures and fittings.

Relaxed in each other's company, the conversation flowed naturally. It had been a long time since she had been out, and she realised how much she had missed some company.

'I'm sorry to put a dampener on things, Lisa, but this beer's lousy. How's your lager?' he whispered.

'Lousy.' She screwed up her face and put her glass on the table. 'Tastes like it's been watered down.'

He leant forward, looked around and said, 'Explains a few things; like, why it's so quiet in here.'

She leant forward and exaggerated her mouth movements as she said, 'I didn't want to mention it at first, but it smells pretty rank in here, too; you must have noticed, and we're not even sat anywhere near the loos.'

As they laughed, she examined his face closely and saw he came to life more when he was happy. 'Do you fancy going to the cinema or grabbing something to eat instead?' she said with her fingers crossed underneath the table. 'My other plans can wait. To be honest they're not important.'

He did not need to be asked twice. He stood up and put on his jacket. 'Let's find somewhere to eat first and then go on to the cinema after if you're not too tired.'

Always the gentleman, he paid the bill every time they went out and appeared insulted if she made any suggestion to pay or split the bill.

Several weeks later, he started to stay over a couple of nights a week and slept on the sofa, initially. Despite her telling him that she coped financially, he still gave her money to help with the bills.

A few months passed. She realised her feelings were more than a crush. She had fallen in love with him and had found her soulmate. He became her whole world and she ached when she was not with him. He was the first thing she thought about when she woke in the mornings and the last thing she thought about before she went to sleep. And when she was not with him, she counted down the hours until she saw him again.

One evening, while they watched the television, he got up from the sofa, while the adverts were on, to make them both a drink.

As he walked back through with a tray in his hands, which had upon it two cups, a plate of digestive biscuits and a little black box, he appeared nervous. He placed the tray on the coffee table, picked up the box and knelt on one knee in front of her.

Her heart started to race with anticipation. She crossed her fingers and toes.

'I know we haven't been together long, but I feel like we're soulmates.' He opened the box and took out a thin gold band with a single diamond. 'Will you make me an even happier man and do me the honour of becoming my wife?' He held out the ring in front of him.

There was an uncomfortable silence while she repeated his question in her head and to check she was not in a dream. 'Yes, of course, I will.' She held out her left hand. He slipped the ring on to her fourth finger. The fit was perfect. He got to his feet and pulled her up from the sofa. They hugged and kissed. A tear of happiness rolled down her cheek, touched his face and got trapped between them.

She reached for a tissue from the dispenser on the coffee table and tried to wipe her smudged mascara from his cheeks. She used several more to clean her own face and to blow her nose in an unladylike manner.

He sat beside her and held her hand. 'I'd like us to move into a place of our own. We could rent somewhere first and move in together before we get married. Is that okay with you? What do you think? You must tell me if you think I'm rushing you into something you're not ready to do.'

Overwhelmed and lost for words, she did not answer. Instead, she grinned, stretched her left arm out in front of her and admired her diamond.

A couple of months later they moved into a lovely new house in a friendly neighbourhood where everyone looked out for each other.

His family and friends donated furniture as the couple tried to save for a deposit on a house of their own. Along with her old furniture, she took the recipe book, with its broken spine, to their new home. He loved when she cooked and baked. He had numerous favourites. But her shepherd's pie and her fruit scones were top of his list.

A couple of years later they asked a couple of work colleagues to be their witnesses and got married at the local register office. They honeymooned in the Lake District and did not leave each other's sides for the whole week.

When they returned from their honeymoon, she was promoted to assistant-manager. Work paid her college fees so she could study for a management qualification, part-time. Her career and homelife were on track and her dreams had started to fall into place.

On the cold evenings when she was not at college, they snuggled up on the sofa, in front of the fire, and caught-up on what had happened during the day before they watched television and went up to bed.

She liked to soak in the bath with a row of lit candles beside her and a glass of red wine to hand; her idea of heaven and no better way to relax; however, he often hinted she should shower more to save money.

They had two spare bedrooms for when family and friends wanted to stay over. Their bedroom was warm and cosy; had a king-size bed with a soft mattress and scatter cushions. The curtains and bedding matched. A deep piled carpet was soft under foot.

It was not long after they were married, she wanted to start a family. She dropped hints for months. At first, her words were ignored until eventually he gave into the idea. They tried for months but were unsuccessful and started to drift apart.

He started a new administration job, out of town, in the council offices. At the interview, he was told the post would progress on to a management role in time. He wanted that promotion but needed to put the hours in and started to get home from work late more often.

She did not want to give up on him or the idea of a baby and she tried to get close to him again.

He arrived home from work one evening and as he walked through the doorway, he looked distant with the look of a man with the world on his shoulders.

She greeted him in the hallway. 'I've cooked one of your favourites for dinner. It's in the oven keeping warm.' She longed for the old days when he used to rush through the door and greet her with a long kiss and a hug.

Her cheerfulness was met with cold rejection. 'Thanks, but I'm not hungry. I might go and have a shower and fall straight into bed.'

She put on her oven gloves, got his dinner from the oven, and scraped the food into the bin. She did not hold back her tears, which flooded out, as she put the plate into the dishwater. The closeness they once shared had been replaced by distance and made it feel like they were strangers.

With the backs of her fingers, she wiped away her tears and made her way upstairs. She got undressed and put on her nightwear, laid in bed, and waited for him to come out of the bathroom. It seemed like an age before he turned off the shower. She heard him brush his teeth with his electric toothbrush and gargle with mouthwash. *He showers every morning, so why does he sometimes shower at night as well? He doesn't overexert himself at work or go to the gym, so he doesn't work up a sweat. And why's he started to get home later more often and acting so distant towards me?*

He came out of the bathroom, turned off the light and got into his side of the bed. He turned on his side so his back was to her.

The bathroom's extractor fan stopped whirring.

'I'm sorry, Steven.' She placed her hand on his shoulder, felt a lump in her throat and held back more tears.

He closed his eyes. 'What for?' There was a coldness to his tone.

She moved closer and pressed her body against his. 'For putting you under so much pressure about us trying for a baby.' She rested her chin on his arm and put her arm around him.

91

'It's okay.' He stayed still. 'I'm just tired and need to get some sleep.'

Rather than annoy him further, she laid back down, turned her back on him and curled up into a ball.

Sometime later, they slept.

The alarm clock's shrill noise woke her the following morning. She reached across to turn it off. His side of the bed felt cold. She got up, put on her dressing gown, went downstairs, and checked the hallway. His jacket and shoes were gone.

Work dragged that day. She was unable to concentrate and looked forward to home time so she could see him again.

That evening, she laid on the sofa and fell asleep as she watched the television. She was woken with a start when the sofa jolted. It felt like someone had kicked the end of it. She sat upright and looked around, but no one was there. 'Steven?' she called out. But she knew she was alone and there would be no response because the house felt empty. She looked up at the wall clock. The time read almost ten thirty. She reached across for her mobile and checked there were no missed calls or messages. The landline had not rung as its ring would have woken her. She wanted to contact him, but he had asked her not to because all his work calls and emails were monitored.

She made her way upstairs, went into the bathroom, cleaned her teeth, and had a wash. She got undressed, put on her pyjamas, and got into bed. The smell of the clean bed linen made her feel comfortable and as soon as her head hit the pillow, she fell asleep.

She was woken after a good night's sleep when her mobile alerted her to a text message. She looked at the alarm clock. Its shrill noise was due to fill the air. She reached across and switched it off before it had chance. His side of the bed had not been slept in.

The message was from Steven. She rubbed her eyes and tried to focus. **Sorry I didn't make it home last night. Stopped at Bob's. Late one at the office. Wasn't sure if you'd gone to bed. Didn't want to wake you.** Much to her annoyance, she was not allowed to respond.

After much consideration, she rang the doctors to make an appointment while she ate lunch. She needed to know the reason she struggled to get pregnant. She rang from the big, comfortable, leather chair in the conference room; ensured the door was in clear view in case she was interrupted.

After several attempts of an engaged tone, her patience paid off and she got through. She cleared her throat. 'Could I make an appointment to see a doctor, please?' She was not sure why she felt nervous.

'Could I take your name?' the receptionist said with an exaggerated telephone voice.

'Yes, my name's Lisa Brook.' She checked the door to make sure no one was there.

'What would you like to see the doctor about? Is it an urgent matter?'

Shocked by the receptionist's rudeness, she paused for a moment before she said, 'It's a personal matter. Something I'd rather discuss with my doctor if you don't mind.' She was puzzled by the receptionist's last question. 'Not sure what you meant when you asked if it's urgent.'

'Is it life threatening?'

93

Lisa took a deep breath. 'Well, no, but it's important.' She had wanted to answer with something witty but felt sorry for the receptionist; maybe she had been in the same job for a long time and was ready for a change.

'I can fit you in to see Doctor Blackthorn in a couple of days.' The receptionist's attitude had improved. 'Would that be convenient?'

'Yes, that'd be good, thank you.' Lisa smiled.

'So, that's Thursday at ten a.m.,' the receptionist said.

'Thank you.'

There was no improvement at home: Steven left early for work every morning and got home late most nights. She had not wanted to add to his worries, so she kept the doctor's appointment to herself and kept busy with work and chores around the home until then.

The doctor ran half an hour behind schedule, which was normal according to other patients who grumbled in the waiting room. Every time the receptionist put down the telephone, it rang straightaway. Every available seat was taken. Three children sat on the floor, in the corner of the room, in a play area with scattered toys and books around them. An old man, who had forgotten what it was like to be young, scowled at them because they made too much noise and were not sat still.

Lisa had browsed through the magazines, read every wall poster, and analysed the diagrams of various illnesses. She had tried to memorise the symptoms of meningitis when the buzzer sounded, and her name was called.

The receptionist looked across at her and pointed down the corridor. 'Lisa Brook for Doctor Blackthorn.'

She looked sterner than she had sounded over the telephone.

Lisa clasped her handbag in front of her as she got to her feet. She made her way along the corridor, looked on each door for Doctor Blackthorn's nameplate, knocked twice and waited.

'Come in,' a well-spoken, gentle, voice said.

As she entered and closed the door behind her, she noticed the doctor was an attractive young man. Not her usual type with his fair hair. There was a silver framed picture on his desk, presumably of his wife, who was also attractive. More posters with diagrams of various internal organs decorated one wall. A bookshelf crammed with medical reference books was against another.

The doctor, who was sat behind his desk, looked up at her. His smile was as warm and caring as his voice. 'Don't look so nervous. Please come in and take a seat, Lisa.' He gestured. 'How can I help you today?'

She sat and composed herself. 'Good morning.' She cleared her throat. 'I'll get straight to the point. I'm concerned that my husband and I are having problems conceiving. We've been trying for several months now.'

'Okay, let's start at the beginning. I must make you aware that it does take some couples a long time to get pregnant. There might not necessarily be any underlying problems. It may simply be a question of giving it more time. Sometimes, it's just some couples try too hard. In my opinion it's too early for me to refer you to a fertility specialist.' He paused and noted she appeared to listen intently before he continued, 'I'll need to ask you a few questions; although, it might have been easier if your husband was with you.'

Her mind had wandered. She had missed half of what he had said. A motorbike sped past on the main road and interrupted her thoughts.

'Are you okay, Lisa?' He frowned. 'I think I lost you for a moment. I hope I didn't offend you when I spoke about your husband.'

She stared at him blankly with her teeth rested on her bottom lip.

'I simply meant sometimes it's easier to speak to both partners together.' Wide-eyed, he looked for some type of sign from her. 'Would you like us to continue, or would you prefer to come back at a later date?'

'Sorry, doctor.' She paused and then nodded. 'I'm fine to continue.'

'If, you're sure.'

She smiled.

He picked up, what looked to be, an expensive pen and made notes on a pad. 'Are your periods regular or irregular?'

'They're regular.' She was not sure if the room had got warmer or if her obvious attraction to him had made her flush.

'It's getting a bit warm in here. Do you mind if I open a window?' he rose from his chair, turned round, and reached up.

'No, not at all. I thought it was me.' While his attention was averted, she ogled him. His jacket had risen, and she could see the outline of his bottom through his close-fitting trousers: small and toned. His broad shoulders gave him a triangular physique.

He took off his jacket, draped it over the back of his chair and sat back down. The armpits of his shirt had dampened. 'Where were we? Oh yes. Do you smoke or have you ever smoked?'

She shook her head and tried to refocus. 'No, I've never smoked.'

'How many units of alcohol would you say you drink in an average week?'

She turned her thoughts to how boring she must sound and wondered if that was why Steven had lost interest in her. 'Not much. The occasional glass of wine.'

He nodded and smiled to himself. 'And you keep yourself healthy? Plenty of exercise?'

'Yes, I'd like to think I was reasonably healthy. I do plenty of walking.'

'I can see from your records you're not on any prescribed medication.' He looked up from his notetaking. 'Do you take anything which isn't prescribed?'

'No, nothing.' She shook her head and looked out of the window. A group of teenagers played truant. Without a care in the world, they smoked and laughed as they tried to push each other into the road.

'I can also see from your records you haven't been pregnant before. Can you tell me if you experience any problems when you have sexual intercourse?' He looked up for a moment to check she had heard.

She shook her head and frowned. 'Not that I can think of.'

He noticed her confusion and rephrased his question. 'Is it painful or do you get a burning sensation when you urinate?'

'No.'

'There's no reason to look so worried, Lisa. Those were routine questions I needed to ask. I'd like to examine you if that's okay; see if anything untoward stands out.' He stood up, made his way towards the door, and opened it. 'If you could go into the examination room.' He pointed to the door across the corridor. 'Are you all right for me to examine you or would you prefer a female to do it?'

'It's fine for you to do it, doctor. Thank you.' She felt more concerned she had wasted the doctor's time than why she struggled to get pregnant.

As she sat on the edge of the examination bed, she looked around the room. The bedside curtain was pulled to one side on the rail. The room was sparsely furnished: a chair, a waste bin, and a storage cabinet. There were no posters or anything of interest on the walls to look at.

Light on his feet, he entered the room and closed the door behind him. 'Could you loosen your jeans and lay on the bed?' He gave her a moment, rubbed his hands together to warm them, pulled her T-shirt up to her navel and started to examine her pelvic area.

She held her breath and tensed up. His fingers felt cool as he moved them across her skin and pushed down in random places.

'Everything feels to be okay. There doesn't appear to be anything obvious to worry about.' He looked down at her and smiled as she laid still on the bed. 'I've noticed from your notes you don't appear to have had a smear test. It's a procedure you may find a little uncomfortable, but it's necessary. If you agree, I'll ask the nurse to come in. She'll perform the test and take a swab sample. She'll also take a blood sample from you and a urine sample. If you don't hear from us within the next couple of weeks, you can assume everything's okay.'

'Thank you, doctor.' She gulped.

'You're welcome, Lisa.' He sanitized his hands, left the room, and closed the door behind him.

Although the window blinds were closed, the room appeared much darker than the doctor's office as though it was dark outside. Her palms were sweaty. Her heart beat faster and she had a fluttery butterfly sensation in the pit of her stomach. She was undecided if to grab her handbag and run.

Too late. There was no escape. The nurse, who was a young woman with an acne scarred face, entered the room. Not one for small talk, she gently carried out a swab test and the smear test and made an uncomfortable situation more bearable.

Lisa put her knickers back on while the nurse washed her hands. The blood sample and urine test were a little less awkward.

After her appointment, she went straight back to work and worked through her lunch break to make up the time. Although relieved she had seen the doctor, she knew the following days would be an anxious wait.

Steven arrived home earlier than expected that evening. He smiled as he walked through the doorway. He appeared more relaxed than he had been during the previous weeks. Was their rocky patch over?

'Hi, how was your day at work?' she said as she made her way towards him.

'A little less stressful.' They embraced. He kissed her cheek. 'And you?' He hung up his jacket and crouched to unfasten his laces.

'It was okay.' She had not intended to tell him about her appointment until she had got her results, but she blurted it out, 'I went to see the doctor this morning.' She wanted to talk to him about everything that had happened over the last few weeks.

'Is everything all right?' He placed his shoes on to the rack. 'You never mentioned you were going to see the doctor.' He straightened up and looked her in the eye.

'I didn't want to bother you. You've been so busy. I'm worried about not being able to get pregnant. I feel such a failure, and I've let you down too.' She felt like she might burst if she did not release her feelings. She longed for them to be close again and loved him more than when they first met.

'It's still early days.' He placed his hands on her shoulders. 'You need to be more patient. I bet the doctor told you the same.'

She looked at him through teary eyes. Deep down, she knew he did not feel the same about her any more from the way he looked at her. It was like he was somewhere else and did not want to return. 'It's all I seem to think about nowadays. It's become an obsession. Taken over my life. You do still want us to have a baby, don't you? Our own little family.'

'What did the doctor say?' He held her face, closed his eyes and kissed her lips.

She felt herself weaken like she was under his spell. 'Pretty much what you've just said. I've had some tests done, so we'll wait and see what comes back.' She took a deep breath and sighed because she knew the doctor and Steven were right.

'I'm sure everything'll be okay, Lisa,' he said. 'Why don't you go and have one of your candlelit baths and I'll fetch a large glass of wine up for you. If you're lucky, I'll even wash your back.' He manoeuvred her towards the stairs and patted her bottom as she stepped on to the bottom stair.

The bubbles were almost over the sides as she laid back in the bath after he had lathered her back. The glass of wine made her drowsy to the point she had to stop herself from falling asleep. She listened to the birds outside the window and tried to remember the last time she felt so relaxed.

A few days later, while she was on her lunch break, she checked her mobile. The doctors' receptionist had left a voicemail for her to make an appointment as soon as possible.

As she made her way towards the conference room to return the call, she feared the worst. *They must have found something; but what? The doctor said they would be in touch if there was anything wrong and it must be serious if they want to see me quickly.*

Rested against the edge of the table, she did not have long to wait until her call was picked up. 'Hi, it's Lisa Brook. You left a message on my mobile. I need to make an appointment to see Doctor Blackthorn as soon as possible, please.'

A younger lady, than the earlier receptionist, with a more pleasant manner, spoke, 'Thanks for ringing back, Lisa. I can fit you in this afternoon at four fifteen. Will that be convenient for you?'

'Yes, I should be able to finish work early.' She took a deep breath. 'Can you tell me, is it something serious?'

'Sorry, I don't know. Doctors don't divulge patients' cases with us. I was simply asked to contact you.' The receptionist wished she could have helped more.

Lisa's life crumbled with that visit to the doctor. As she sat in the waiting room, she heard nothing but her own rapid heartbeat and heavy breathing. Something was wrong, but was it life-threatening? How long did she have left to live? She prepared herself for the worst.

Baffled by how she was sat in the doctor's office, she could not recall the receptionist call out her name or her walk along the corridor.

'The smear test results aren't available yet. They should be with you within the next few days. You should receive them in the post.' His eyebrows lowered as he paused. 'However, the other test results have come back and I'm afraid to tell you that you've tested positive for chlamydia.'

She had only heard snippets of what he had said but caught the last word. Should she be relieved or scared? Was it a common illness or a rare disease which only one in a million contracted? She looked at the doctor for reassurance. 'Sorry, I've not heard of it before. What is it?'

'It's a sexually transmitted infection. You can carry it for a long time without realising and not show any symptoms whatsoever. But if it's left untreated it can cause problems, including infertility.' He scribbled on his prescription pad. 'I'm going to put you on a course of strong antibiotics. I'd advise you not to drink alcohol while you're taking them, or they might become ineffective. You'll need to come back in three months, so we can check the antibiotics have worked. I know you're trying for a baby but if you could please have protected sex until we give you the all-clear.'

'It's not possible, doctor. I think there's been some sort of mistake, maybe a mix-up with my results. I can assure you I *do not* sleep about. Steven is the only person I've ever slept with. I know he had a few sexual partners before we got together, but he assured me he'd been checked at a clinic before we slept together, and he was given the all-clear.' She stared at the doctor and waited for him to apologise.

'You have chlamydia. There's been no mistake or mix-up,' he said. 'Although the damage to men is not as bad as it can be for women, you'll still need to tell your husband as soon as possible so he can get the treatment he needs.' He tore the prescription from the pad and handed it to her. 'You need to start taking these as soon as you can.'

Her head spun and her stomach churned. She felt foolish. Why had she been rude? 'Thank you, doctor.' She smiled.

He nodded. 'I'll see you soon. Take care, Lisa.'

When she got home, she picked up the post from the hallway mat and made her way into the kitchen. She threw the post on to the worktop. Normally, she would have looked through the post first and put any junk mail into the bin. She made herself a cup of tea, sat down and stared out of the window. She tried to clear her mind and keep calm.

Steven arrived home from work. He was a little earlier than usual again.

She stayed seated in the kitchen; listened as he closed the door behind him; pictured him as he took off his jacket and shoes in his usual manner.

He did not check if she was at home or ask how she was or how her day had been. 'I'm going to have a quick shower before dinner,' he said before he made his way upstairs. He did not wait for her to respond.

From the bottom of the stairs, she heard the shower running. His mobile pinged beside her. She rummaged through the pockets of his jacket and found his mobile in the breast pocket. Someone called Olivia had sent him a text. She did not recognise the name. He had never mentioned anyone by that name. She scrolled through and saw most of the messages were from Olivia. She opened the text. It read: **Hi, S. Sorry I couldn't make our rendezvous this evening. Had to get home to Mark. You know what he gets like. Love you, darling xxx**.

As bile rose in her throat, the top stair creaked. She did not look up, but knew he was there. She did not have time to put the mobile back into his pocket. 'Thought you were having a shower.' She was unsure as to why she was the one who felt guilty.

'I was coming to get my mobile,' he said as he descended the stairs.

'Do you love her, Steven?'

He turned round, made his way back upstairs and turned off the shower before he joined her in the kitchen. His mobile was on the worktop with Olivia's message displayed.

'Do you love her, this Olivia, whoever she is?' She would not allow him to carry on with someone else behind her back. She had promised herself she would not get tearful. All she wanted was the truth. She was surprised by how strong she felt. 'Please, Steven, answer my question. I'm asking you nicely. I promise I won't kick off. You owe me that much at least.'

'Yes, I do, but I love you too.' His eyes welled up.

'How long's it been going on?'

He felt cornered and looked down at the floor. 'Not long.'

'How long, Steven?' Why did he continue to treat her like a fool? She felt a spark of anger ignite inside.

He slithered down to the floor and leant against a cabinet with his legs outstretched in front of him. 'I've been seeing her, off and on, for about five years.' His eyes widened as he realised how deceitful his confession sounded.

'Five years!' She gaped. 'I'm confused.' She shook her head. 'That's longer than we've been together. Who the hell is she?'

'I met her at work. She was the receptionist at a company I used to work for.' Like a child, he put his knees up to his chest and hugged them.

Rain lashed against the window. A chill made the hairs on her arms and the back of her neck stand on end. 'Why did you bother with me if you were already seeing someone else? Don't you think you should have told me you weren't available?'

He got to his feet, turned round, and looked out of the window. 'Wasn't that easy.'

'Really?' She watched his reflection in the window and knew he watched her too. 'Why? Seems simple enough to me.' She wanted to throw something at him; instead, she clasped her hands together.

'Because she's married and she's an older woman with children. She won't leave him because he's got money. He can give her stuff which I can't afford.'

'Oh, I get it.' She got up from her chair and made her way towards the kettle. 'You're with me because you can't have her. In other words, you're stuck with me.'

He stood behind her, put his arms around her waist and kissed her neck. 'I'm not stuck with you. Don't you understand, Lisa? I love you.'

She turned round, sneered, and pushed him away. 'I went back to the doctor's today for my results. I've got an STI, which *you* must have given me.'

'An STI.' He gaped and took a step back. 'What STI?'

'Chlamydia! So, you'll need to make an appointment to see your doctor for treatment.' She was unsure if she should feel sorry for him or laugh at his facial expression. 'Please remember to give Olivia a personal thank you from me.'

'Are you sure this STI's something I've given you?'

'You cheeky bastard! You're unbelievable, do you know that? How dare you?' She started to cry.

'I'm sorry, Lisa. You were never supposed to find out. I didn't set out to hurt you.' He reached out to her and moved closer. 'You've got to believe me. Where do we go from here?'

'I don't know.' She rested her head against his chest. He put his arms around her and held her close. Despite everything, she still loved him. 'I don't know about anything anymore.' She raised her head and looked him in the eye. Her eyes were bloodshot and tired. 'Our relationship's based on a lie. You've lied to me from the start, and I don't mind admitting that I hurt. I feel like you've ripped my heart out and I don't know if it'll ever heal.'

'Please give me a chance.' He kissed her forehead. 'We could start again.' His sweet breath blew over her face.

She shrugged. 'I don't know.' She shook her head. 'I need time to think. What about Olivia? Every time you're not with me or you're late, I'll think you're with her.' She paused. 'I had to check your mobile tonight; I've never felt the need to do that before.'

'I promise I'll end it with her.'

She turned her back on him, put a teabag into her cup and poured in hot water from the kettle. 'Go and have your shower.'

'Will you still be here when I come back down?'

'Yes, I'll still be here.' With a teaspoon, she scooped the teabag out of her cup and made her way towards the refrigerator to get the milk. 'I've not got anywhere else to go, have I?'

For several weeks tensions were high in the Brook household; a mixture of betrayal and hurt. They lived separate lives. He managed to get home early, every evening, for a couple of weeks, but it was not long until he started to arrive home late again. She felt disappointed, but never questioned him; already aware he had betrayed her again as the smell of Olivia's perfume on him was too strong to mask. Why had she never noticed before?

One evening, she sat at the kitchen table with the local evening paper open. She looked through the properties to rent section and wondered if it should be her or him who left.

He popped his head through the doorway. 'I'm nipping down to the Duck and Drake for a couple.' Their local pub: a place they often went when they first got together.

Part of her wanted to jump up and go with him, so they could reminisce about old times and try to reignite their relationship, but she knew it was over. 'Okay.' She noted his pale complexion and the dark circles around his glazed over eyes. She had a strong sense of déjà vu. As he turned to leave, she got to her feet to inspect the floor beside him. When she saw the five small black shadows, she knew his fate was out of her hands.

She felt scared and alone when she went up to bed that night because she knew she would never see him alive again.

*

Steven had made his way towards the Duck and Drake down the footpath towards the bridge. Nettles poked through the overgrown grass to both sides and stung his legs through his trousers.

The downpour had stopped. A rapid flowed beneath the bridge. Branches and twigs, which the wind had brought down, rode on the river's surface.

In a trance, he stepped on to the bridge: an old metal structure with a concrete slabbed path which had stood the test of time through many rough winters. He climbed up on to the top rail, somehow balanced, stretched his arms out to the sides and stared ahead. He fell forward and momentarily hovered in the air, like a bird who waited to attack its prey, before he bellyflopped into the river. He had always been a good swimmer, but he made no effort to save himself as he surrendered to the strong current and put his face beneath its surface.

The day after, Lisa reported him missing. The police found his body a day later. She was upset but not shocked.

A couple of weeks after his funeral, she received a letter from his solicitor. Unbeknown to her, he had made a will. She had been left all his belongings, which included a life insurance policy; a tidy sum which she had no prior knowledge of. She arranged for the monies to be transferred into her account.

A few weeks later, as she sorted through his belongings, she found a scratch card in the inner pocket of a suit jacket. She threw the card on to the bed and did not scratch it until later after she had eaten dinner.

Numerous times she checked the card. It was a definite winner; three amounts matched: fifty thousand pounds.

Chapter Six

A Fresh Start

Lisa's priorities changed after Steven's passing. A management roll at the call centre no longer seemed important. She had almost completed her course at college but decided to drop out because it was not for her any more. She had learned plenty but felt life was too short and she wanted more from it. The loneliness she could cope with. The memories, good and bad, at work and at home, were a different matter. Everywhere she looked, there were reminders, sometimes gentle and sometimes not so, a tune on the radio or a certain smell.

After Doctor Blackthorn had given her the all-clear, she made plans to move away. With the money Steven and she had saved, his life insurance and the scratch card win, she got her thoughts together and made her final decision on where to move to.

She visited the Lake District every weekend to browse the estate agents' windows and view properties. The weeks soon passed. She was kept busy as she house-hunted, worked her notice, and packed up her belongings ready for the move.

The Lake District's beautiful scenery had always fascinated her. The pace of life there was one where she had time to appreciate what nature intended. Every time she visited, she felt more at home; knew it was where she belonged.

She bought a one-bedroom, open-plan, apartment and had money left in the bank.

On the eve of the moving day, her excitement and anxiety made it impossible for her to sleep.

She got up early on moving day, ate breakfast, showered, and made sure everything was packed away before she had a final clean around.

Her landline had been disconnected. She had arranged for her post to be redirected, had notified everyone who needed to know about her move and had taken final water, electric and gas meter readings.

After a final check of her to-do list, she sat on a chair arm in the living room, stared out of the window and waited for the removal men to arrive.

The removal men, who reminded her of a modern-day Laurel and Hardy, arrived punctually, and took over; much to her relief. They did not stop for a rest and soon had the house emptied. They got into their van and were on their way.

She stood in the living room for a moment. Did she have any regrets? Not only was the house empty of furniture but also of the life she had once shared with Steven. With mixed feelings of sadness and excitement, she walked from room to room to check nothing had been left behind. Each room gave her unique memories, both good and bad.

For the last time, she closed the front door behind her and walked to the estate agents to hand in the keys.

Her train was delayed, but the rest of the journey ran smoothly.

When she arrived at her new home, she saw the removal men in their van. The driver had his head rested against the seat's headrest; his mouth open as he napped. His colleague's feet were up on the dashboard as he read a newspaper and ate a sandwich. He looked across at her. She waved and went up to the apartment to unlock the door.

The apartment was on the middle floor of five, had recently been decorated, fitted with modern appliances, and had underfloor heating in the bathroom.

She had looked forward to a fresh start where no one knew her. Apart from Susan and her family, no one else knew where she had intended to move to. She had given Elizabeth her telephone number in case she wanted to stay in touch, but she would not hold her breath.

When she entered, she was greeted by a faint cigar smell. She thought it strange because when she had originally looked around the apartment, the estate agent told her no one had ever lived there. She opened a couple of windows.

The removal men finished their break and took the awkward, heavier items up to the apartment first. She propped the door open for them and made her way down to their van to collect the box which she had marked up *kettle*. The same box contained cups, coffee, teabags, and sugar. She had bought a pint of milk from the train station shop when she arrived. She rinsed out three cups and made them all a hot drink.

When all the furniture and boxes had been unloaded into the right rooms, she paid the removal men with a cheque, thanked them for their hard-work and locked the door behind them. She leant against the back of the door and smiled as she looked around her new home. All she had to do was empty the boxes and put her belongings into place.

She picked up the nearest box, placed some of the candles in her bathroom and the pots of green foliage on the windowsills which made the place look homelier.

She emptied box after box until she grew tired. She put her bed together with a screwdriver and an Allen key, dragged the mattress across the floor and lowered it on to the wooden lats. She placed a fitted sheet, pillows with cases, and duvet with cover, on to the bed and laid on top. As she stared at the ceiling, she started to doze but was woken when she saw a shadow out of the corner of her eye; someone had walked past her bedroom door.

She sat up. 'Hello? Is someone there?'

There was no response.

Used to strange happenings, she was not scared as she got up from the bed and went to check if someone was in the apartment with her. Again, she noticed the faint cigar smell.

So as not to disturb any possible intruder and to catch them off-guard, she tiptoed around her apartment. She checked the living room first: clear. The bathroom and kitchen were also clear. She was alone.

She slept well that night.

The following morning, the sound of twittering birds outside her window woke her.

She pulled back a curtain and looked down. A small group of people exercised, and a dog walker watched over her dog as it pooped.

The sun would soon burn away the cloud cover.

Lisa needed to buy groceries. She was hungry as she had not eaten much the day before. She got dressed in the same clothes she had worn the day before and headed out of the door. It was still early and no one else appeared to be awake in the block.

The nearest shop was around the corner. The goods were expensive, so she bought two croissants, a jar of jam and the local newspaper which featured the job vacancies. She would look around later for a supermarket.

A week later, after she had unpacked and settled in, she found a part-time job in a local bed and breakfast: Woodhayes. The owners, June, and Barry Hayes were a middle-aged couple. Her maiden name was Wood. They merged these surnames to name their business.

Lisa worked mornings. She changed the beds, cleaned the rooms, and helped with any other chores when needed. June and Barry soon made her feel like one of the family.

Most of the bed and breakfast guests always appeared in good spirits; well-to-do people with manners; several were regulars.

Lisa was allowed to keep any tips which were left in the rooms and if any of the guests ever left their belongings, she always handed them in to reception.

When you lived in a friendly village it made it easier to meet new people and she felt honoured when she was invited to join a group which went hillwalking every Sunday. The group always finished their walks with dinner and a drink in the local pub: The Red Squirrel. They were mainly a friendly group, and some always had a story to tell. Most were quite a bit older than her, but they were a spritely bunch. On the first few walks she struggled to keep up with them, but it did not take long for her to get used to their pace.

Some of the walkers visited the Lake District every weekend; others on occasion; some were locals. The group always met at the same place and at the same time every week. The number of attendees depended on how many were available; usually between six and twelve.

Some of the walking group members were as follows: Derek had visited the Lakes since he was a child and soon after he was widowed visited most weekends. A pleasant man who liked to tell stories about his late wife, Emma, and how proud he was of his daughter. She was a neurosurgeon who lived in New York and had been given American citizenship. She flew back to visit him occasionally, but he could not afford the airfare to New York and would not take hand-outs from her, as he called them. He missed his wife and daughter and visited the Lakes because he had fond memories of them all there as a family. He treated Lisa like a daughter and was always kind to everyone in the group.

There was Mavis; an obstinate old woman who only went on the walks so she could moan and reiterate how useless the entire male population was. Even though she was local, she did not go with the group too often. Lisa tried not to engage in conversation with her for too long, if she could help it, as she made her feel sad.

Mr Kenneth and Mrs Irene Butterworth were a delightful old couple. They filled Lisa with inspiration. The couple had been married for over fifty years, had never spent a night apart and went everywhere together. Lisa had never heard a cross word exchanged between them. If either of them made a comment, the other always agreed; while some couples she knew tended to bicker and contradict each other. Like most couples they had experienced sorrow in their lives. They had not been able to have children of their own, so they spoilt their many nephews and nieces. Lisa felt sad when she thought how awful it would be when one of them passed away and wondered how the other would cope as the couple had a beautiful kinship which one day would end in such terrible heartache.

Sally worked in the kitchen at Woodhayes Bed and Breakfast. She helped prepare breakfasts and cleaned the dishes. June was insistent the dishes were cleaned the old-fashioned way and not in one of those silly dishwashers. Sally, who was in her early forties, was a pleasant and cheerful woman; although, from stories Lisa had heard from local people, Sally was not someone you got on the wrong side of. She had a partner who she had lived with for a few years, but they lived separate lives; each did their own thing on a Sunday. She liked to go out for walks while her partner stayed-in and played on her games console.

There were two brothers, Adam, and Rob. They were Mavis's nephews and were like chalk and cheese. They never walked with or spoke to Mavis. Lisa discovered they were related to Mavis, by accident, when she overheard others in the group mention it. Adam, who was the oldest by a couple of years, was the mature one. Rob had a cheekiness about him which was difficult to ignore, and he always gave everyone a guided tour of everywhere they went, if they wanted it or not.

Another middle-aged couple went along occasionally. The wife appeared timid while the husband appeared to be her master. He made all the decisions without a word from her. They always kept themselves to themselves and never went for dinner with the others. Even though they were quiet, they always greeted everyone in the group and smiled. Some of the group had labelled them weird, but Lisa preferred to think of them as quiet people who did not want anyone else to know their business.

She looked forward to Sundays because she felt part of the community and met with like-minded friends.

One Sunday, after she had finished dinner, she drank up and decided to head home. She felt wearier than usual, and she had started with a headache. She needed sleep and imagined the warmth of her bed. She had enjoyed the catch-up but concluded that level of lethargy meant either a cold or virus would follow. The Red Squirrel was not far from home, but she still had a little walk.

It was unusually quiet in the village for a Sunday. Probably because the weather had taken a turn for the worse and the skies looked stormy.

As she made her way past the shops, she noticed a tall, well-built man in the reflection of one of the windows. He appeared to look across at her. It had been a long time since a man had paid her any attention. She pretended she had not seen him and looked down at the ground. He drew parallel with her and crossed over the road towards her. She felt a little nervous, found some essential energy and quickened her pace.

'Excuse me, love.' He stopped in front of her and blocked her path. 'Sorry to pester you, but do you have the time on you?'

Even though he was taller than her, she thought the wisp of black hair, which peeked out from underneath his beany hat, made him look cute. He had a friendly face which made her feel calmer. She raised her hand, looked at her watch, and said, 'Yes, of course, it's –' She stopped when she saw him slide his hand into his jacket pocket.

He pulled out a knife, flicked it open and held the blade's tip against her stomach.

She tried to remain calm, but she tensed, and her heart started to race.

His face grew closer to hers. 'We can do this the easy way or the hard way.' He tilted his head to one side. 'Your choice.' He tilted his head to the other side. 'Hand over your money or the blade goes in.' His facial expression stayed the same with no regards for her horror.

Although she wanted to scream for help, she tried to appear brave as she handed him her purse. Their eye contact remained throughout. She felt the blade's tip press against her, and she breathed in.

He snatched the purse from her, opened it and frowned. 'Where's the rest?' He put the knife back into his pocket.

She kept still, breathed deeply, and felt him touch her inappropriately as he rummaged in her pockets.

He grabbed her backpack and tipped the contents on to the ground. A small mirror cracked as it hit the path. A lipstick rolled into the road and a couple of tampons laid alongside her hairbrush. He threw the backpack on to the ground, turned round, and ran with her purse.

As she dropped to the ground and sobbed into her hands, she realised she had wet herself.

There had not been much cash in her purse, and she never carried plastic cards unless she knew she had to go to a cashpoint. She only carried enough money with her which she knew she needed, along with a small emergency surplus. She had always done that; mainly, so she did not overspend and on the off chance something like that happened.

As he ran off, he turned his head to look back at her. His facial expression had not changed; however, his complexion had paled and the darkness around his eyes made them look sunken. He wore the familiar death mask.

She had expected to see small black shadows as she looked down at his feet, but there were none. As if behind schedule, they rose out of the ground beside her, hovered to check she was all right before they soared and pursued him.

She had never felt so scared in her life. She stayed on the ground, hidden in a corner, with her back against a wall, and hugged her knees. She would not move from there until she was sure he had gone.

As she looked around, there was no one to help. She got up from the ground, picked up her backpack and belongings and ran home.

She climbed out of her wet clothes, put them into the washing machine and had a long soak in a hot bubble bath.

Still shaken, she put on her dressing gown before she picked a bottle of red from the wine rack and poured herself a large glass. She sat at the kitchen table, rested her head in her hands and sobbed again.

The following day, she made an excuse not to go into work; told them she was ill. She did not want to talk to anyone about what had happened and knew if she spent the day alone, she would be back to her normal self sooner.

As she laid underneath her duvet, the day appeared to drag. She decided to get up, kept herself busy, and although her apartment was already immaculate, she cleaned every surface from top to bottom.

Later that evening, she regained her appetite and made chicken soup with two slices of toast. She put them on a tray, sat down on the sofa and pointed the remote control at the television. The local news was on.

'On tonight's news. Police are investigating an horrific murder – a possible ritual killing – after finding a man's body last night.' The female newsreader, who had a local accent, always seemed to smile, no matter how bad the headline was. 'And how a local man has raised more money for a local hospice, and what to expect from the weather in the week ahead.'

Intrigued, Lisa continued to watch as she put a spoonful of soup into her mouth. The soup was still too hot and burnt her tongue. She took the spoon out again and blew on it to cool it down before she slurped it.

A photograph of the man who had mugged her the day before filled the screen. She closed her eyes, opened them, and looked at his photograph again. She gulped loudly as she swallowed her soup. She edged forward, placed her tray down on the floor and continued to listen.

'While mountain rescue was coming back from a routine training exercise last night, they noticed something out of the ordinary. Because of the nature of the incident, we have been asked not to show any photographs or films at this time.' The newsreader looked at her laptop, raised her eyebrows, and then gaped. 'It's believed the man's name is Jack Lowe. He's not local to the area. We've been informed that his next of kin have been notified. The naked young man was found hanging upside down with fatal injuries to his body. A nearby smouldering fire contained fragments of clothing, believed to belong to the man. The police are continuing with their investigation. If anyone knows this man or saw anything suspicious, please ring the Crimestoppers number shown on the bottom of the screen.'

Lisa switched off the television, picked up her tray and made her way into the kitchen. She placed the tray on the worktop and made her way into her bedroom.

As she curled up on her bed, she looked across at her bedside cabinet. The purse, which Jack had robbed from her, was on the top.

She picked up the purse and unzipped it. The money was still inside.

*

Once Jack was out of sight, he stopped running. He placed her purse inside his jeans pocket and started to walk.

As if programmed, like a robot, he changed direction and made his way towards the hills; although, he was not dressed appropriately for a hill walk. His pace quickened until he ran. He focused ahead and ignored his surroundings. He slipped a few times but always picked himself up and continued despite the cuts and bruises on his knees and shins. He was not out of breath until he neared the top.

Bewildered as to how he had got there, and out of his trance, he sat down on a boulder. At first, he struggled to catch his breath but remained calm and took deep breaths.

When he tried to get to his feet again, he found he could not move. He looked down at his hands and got the strangest sensation as though his arms were not his own. A black shadow rose from his body and took on human form. 'What the fuck!' he said as he scrambled backwards.

It leant forward and positioned its head in front of his face. 'We can do this the easy way or the hard way. Your choice. Hand over the purse or the blade goes in.'

His eyes widened.

It sensed his fear and fed from his energy.

He took Lisa's purse from out of his pocket and placed it on the ground beside him.

'Stand up.' It stayed close; almost touched him. 'Take off your belt.'

He slowly got to his feet.

It mirrored his every move.

Although no longer under its spell, he decided to follow its orders. He took off his belt and dropped it on the ground beside him.

'Take the knife out of your pocket and place it on the ground.'

He put his hand into his pocket and pulled out the knife. But he did not place it on the ground. Instead, he flicked it open, rushed forward and tried to jab the black shadow.

It roared with laughter as he fell through it.

He landed on a rocky outcrop and tumbled off.

It entered his body before he hit the ground and levitated him on to a ledge. It hovered in front of him; not as close as before, but enough to make him feel uneasy. 'Even though you amuse me, I am not in the mood for your silly games. Be a good chap and put the knife on the ground.' It hovered above him; lowered to his left; moved in front of him to his right and then stopped behind him. 'You do know you are going to die, don't you? I am going to enjoy killing you and the more you try to resist, the harder you make it for yourself.'

He placed the knife on the ground beside him.

An uncomfortable silence followed.

The weather had taken a turn for the worse. Fine rain had soaked through his clothes. The hairs on his arms stood on end as the gentle breeze turned blustery. He twisted his torso to check behind him. Wind blew into his eyes and made them water which made it harder to focus on the black shadow. 'Who are you? More to the point, what are you? And what the hell do you want with me?' His voice trembled.

It stayed quiet for a moment before it said, 'Take off your clothes, Jack.'

He slowly undressed.

As it inclined its head to one side, it noticed his soiled underwear.

'How do you know my name?' He folded his clothes and placed them on to a tidy pile on the ground.

It pushed down on his shoulders. 'Sit down.'

'Please. I'm begging you; tell me what you plan to do to me?'

It had grown bored, wanted to complete its duty and be on its way. 'Silence! No more questions. No more talking.'

He gulped. His breathing became loud and erratic.

Again, it fed from his anxiety. 'Wrap the belt around your ankles and pull it tight.'

He froze for a second. Should he run? No. Where would he go? Instead, he hoped whatever it was that tormented him would change its mind and disappear. He picked up his belt, wrapped it around his ankles, pulled it as tight as he could and then let go.

The belt tightened further. He screamed as he was hoisted into the air, feet first. A nail was pushed through the belt and into a rocky outcrop as though the rock were made of dough.

It hovered upside down in front of him and then roared with laughter before it disappeared.

All was quiet again.

He tried to reach up to untie his belt, but the more he moved, the more the belt tightened. 'Help,' he yelled. His face reddened. His temporal veins bulged and pulsated. 'For fuck's sake will someone *please* help me?' But his cries went unheard. He closed his eyes, exhaled long and audibly and when he inhaled again, he smelt smoke. He opened his eyes and saw a cloud of smoke drift in front of him.

It was then he noticed, through the smoke, that his flick knife hovered in front of him at waist level. He waved his hands in front of him to try to knock the knife out of the way. The knife lunged forward and jabbed him through his hand. It pulled out and then darted forward again; stabbed him above his hip; sliced him across his abdomen.

He passed out and his body hung lifelessly. His intestines peeked through the gash until gravity forced them to spew out. They hung over his face like a blanket.

The black shadow was gone.

*

Lisa decided not to report the mugging to the police. There would be too many questions, and the purse had been returned.

The following day, she went into work and tried to act like nothing had happened. She kept herself busy, spoke only when she was spoken to and smiled when needed.

The murder was the talk of the village. Nothing like that had ever happened there before. When the guests and her colleagues talked about the murder, she did not join in.

After work, she went straight home, locked, and bolted the door behind her.

Chapter Seven

William Oates

The Stuart Morton School of Motoring car pulled up on the street outside Lisa's apartment. Stuart parked in the same place every week. His car stood out with its luminous lime green colour and its signage. A patient middle-aged gentleman, who was her third driving teacher, was always punctual and never let her down. Previous instructors had failed her with various unbelievable excuses. Month after month, she'd had good days and off days, but she would not be beaten; determined she would pass the test no matter how many attempts it took her.

With her jacket and driving shoes already on, she looked out of her window to check in case he had arrived early.

She locked the apartment door behind her, hurried down the stairway and outside. As she opened the driver's door, the heat hit her like she had disembarked an aeroplane on holiday. She got into the car and threw her handbag on to the back seat. 'Hi, Stuart.' She adjusted her seat and mirrors.

'Afternoon, Lisa. How are you today?' He paused. 'There's no need to look so worried, it's only a bit of snow.' He looked up at the sky as though he tried to predict the weather. 'Don't think we're going to get any more yet.'

She smelt whisky on his breath. 'I'm feeling determined. This is going to be a good lesson.' She tried to convince herself as she turned her head to smile at him. 'How are you today?'

'I'm not too bad, thank you. I can't complain. Well, I could, but I don't think anyone would listen.' He was always polite. She had never heard him grumble about anyone or anything. 'I've had the car repaired so if we can avoid bumping into stationary objects today that would be great.'

'Sorry again.' She smiled and shrugged.

'When you're ready, Lisa. I'd like you to pull out and drive down the road.' He made himself comfortable. 'Take it steady. The road might be slippery in places.'

She checked her mirrors, looked over her shoulder and signalled.

He put his arm around the back of her headrest and looked over his shoulder to check.

She pulled out.

'Good.' He nodded. 'If you can drive on a bit further and take the second turning on your left by the old telephone box. We'll drive to one of the side roads up there and practice reversing around the corner.'

She listened carefully and followed his instructions. She had passed her theory test a few weeks before; that was the easy part. She drove forwards okay, but she struggled to reverse.

'That's much better, Lisa. You must be feeling more confident.' His mobile beeped. He checked the message before he continued, 'We'll have another go at that and then we'll have a quick refresher on a three-point turn. I know you're capable. I just want you to practice.'

She handled the car well on the reversing and the three-point turn. She drove back to the main road and further on to another side road.

'I know you haven't done this before but I'm going to show you how to parallel park.'

Her eyes widened. 'Um, right. I'm not sure about that. I don't think I'm ready yet.'

'Trust me. You'll be fine. Simply turn the wheel when I tell you to.'

Her lesson was soon over. He asked her to drive back to her apartment. 'Not bad today. We just need you to have a few more lessons like this one and then you'll be ready for your test.' He paused. 'Same time next week?'

'Please, Stuart, and thank you so much for being so patient with me.' She reached into the back of the car and grabbed her handbag.

He leant across her and switched off the engine. 'Honestly, you've done well today. You need to start believing in yourself. I've had far worse drivers than you and managed to get them through their test. Next lesson, I want to see a more positive attitude from you because I know you'll be okay.'

She nodded, got out, left the driver's door ajar, leant forward, and looked inside the car. 'Bye, Stuart. See you next week.'

Part of her wanted to do a hop, a skip, and a jump as she made her way towards her apartment. Halfway along the path, she turned round and waved at him.

Once inside, she made herself a well-earned drinking chocolate with fresh cream and marshmallows.

The months passed quickly. Her apartment looked different from when she had moved in. She had made a few alterations, decorated the place throughout and there were an abundance of plants and candles.

She still enjoyed her work at Woodhayes Bed and Breakfast. Went for walks on Sundays with the same group of people and had dinner at The Red Squirrel. She loved the routine and her friends; felt like she belonged there.

Until a new member, who had recently moved into the area, joined their walking group, she had not thought about a new relationship. She had not wanted to complicate her life and found it hard to trust anyone new. But she was mesmerised by him. Unsure why, as he was at least ten years older than her. He appeared to be quite shy, kept himself to himself, and never looked or spoke to her the first few times he walked with the group. He did not join them at the pub afterwards either.

A few weeks passed before she picked up the courage to introduce herself. He was stood alone as he waited for other group members to arrive. She saw her opportunity and pounced, 'Hi, I'm Lisa. Pleased to meet you.' She held out her hand and grinned.

His eyebrows raised as he held out his hand. 'Hello, Lisa. I'm William. My friends call me Bill.'

'Hi, Bill. I've seen you a few times. How're you enjoying the group?' she said with a twinkle in her eye.

'Yes, it's good. Well, I must be enjoying it, I keep coming back for more, don't I?'

As she smiled, she heard the familiar chatter of her Sunday afternoon companions as they made their way up the road. She turned round to check.

Most of the group had arrived.

She turned back to Bill who had already set off. 'Do you mind if I walk with you?' she called after him.

He stopped and turned round. 'No, not at all. Might be nice to have a walking buddy.'

She caught up to him and walked alongside him.

The walk was quiet, and it was not long until the group had arrived at the hill tops. They stopped to take in the breath-taking views.

Lisa poured herself a tea from her flask. 'Would you like some?' she said to Bill before she took a sip.

'No, I'm fine, thank you.' He continued to admire the views.

'Doesn't the snow make the scenery look more breath-taking?'

'It certainly does.'

'I could stand here forever especially when it's a sunny day, too. You've got to make the most of days like today.' She chatted away, oblivious to his need for peace and quiet. 'I think it's forecast to be sunny for most of the week; hope it doesn't make the snow melt too quickly.'

He realised they had a shared interest in not only walking but also nature and he turned his head to look at her. 'No, that would be a shame.'

She was keen to learn more about him. 'How long have you lived round here?'

'Not long; a few months.' As though self-conscious, he looked away.

She reached into her backpack, got out a pen and wrote down her number in the corner of a magazine. 'In case you need to get in touch or need advice about anything local.' She tore off the number and passed the scrap of paper to him. 'Get in touch anytime.'

He smiled, took the scrap of paper, and put it in his jacket pocket.

The group made their way back towards the village. Lisa walked alongside Bill. 'Why don't you come and have Sunday dinner at our local with the rest of us. I'm always starving by the time we've finished walking. They do a tasty roast; reasonably priced too,' she said, unable to contain her enthusiasm. 'Unless you've got somewhere else you need to be.'

'Sounds tempting. It'd be rude to say no, wouldn't it?'

He did not say much as they ate. He was polite and answered questions he was asked and smiled when someone said something funny. He still chewed his food as he stood up and put on his jacket. 'My apologies, I'm going to have to make tracks. I've got a few jobs I need to sort out before I go back to work tomorrow. I'll see you all next week.' He smiled and waved. Some waved and others said goodbye. 'It's been good talking with you, Lisa.'

She tried to hide her disappointment as she waved.

He was in her thoughts, a lot, the following week. She looked out for him when she went out and ensured she wore enough make-up in case she bumped into him.

He was not there the following Sunday. Had she scared him off? Been too forward?

She had been right to feel hopeful for the following week. He walked ahead of her. She hurried and caught up to him. 'Hi, Bill.'

'Hi ... Sorry, I've forgotten your name.' He blushed.

'Lisa!' Her smile faded and her pace slowed. She would let him walk ahead if he wanted.

He slowed down and turned his head to continue with their conversation, 'Sorry, Lisa. How are you? I'm useless with names. I hope you'll forgive me.'

'Don't worry about it.' She forgave his lapse of memory and tucked her hair behind her ears. 'I'm good. What about you?'

'Not too bad, thanks. I needed to get out for a long walk today. It'll do me the power of good.' His strides grew longer, and his pace quickened.

In the weeks that followed, they grew closer; walked and chatted every Sunday.

'Will you be joining us for dinner today?'

'Sounds great. I missed breakfast.' He rubbed his stomach in a circular motion.

'Good, because it's your turn to buy the wine.' She raised an eyebrow.

After the group had eaten, it was Lisa's turn to leave early as she had an earlier start the following morning. She grabbed her backpack and jacket and said her goodbyes.

Bill stood up, put on his jacket, and followed her towards the door. When they reached the door, he put his hand on her shoulder. 'Would it be okay if we went back to yours for coffee?'

'Yes, of course.'

He held the door open. 'Lead the way.' He followed her out.

They talked and laughed. Not long after they were back at her apartment. The climb up the stairway was harder on a full stomach and after a long walk. They caught their breath as she unlocked the door.

He took off his shoes, hung up his jacket and glanced around. 'Nice place you have here.'

'Thank you. I like it.' She made her way towards the kitchen and switched on the kettle.

As she showed him around, she explained everything she had done to the place and went into fine detail about her do-it-yourself skills.

They sat down on the sofa and drank their coffees. Time flew as they talked of how to solve society's problems.

He looked at his watch and made a face. 'I'd better get going so you can have that early night you wanted. Thanks for the coffee.' She took his cup from him and showed him to the door. He put on his shoes and jacket, leant forward, and kissed her cheek. She blushed. He cupped her chin, lifted her face, and smiled. 'I'll see you next Sunday.'

'I'll look forward to it.' She stared at his lips before she leant forward, closed her eyes, and kissed him.

As the weeks went by, he confided in her more. Explained how he had been hurt, more than once, in past relationships and that was the reason he wanted to take it slowly. He was a thoughtful lover and made her feel wanted and special. She had fallen for him and was in love all over again.

A steady flow of hand-delivered flowers arrived at her work and home. She had never received flowers before. At first, she felt overwhelmed. He wrote her poetry and left the verses in strategic places, so she would find them when he was not there.

Almost a year had passed before she pushed the commitment subject. 'Please stay over tonight. It would be nice to see you laid next to me when I wake in the morning.' She rested her head on his shoulder, looked him in the eye and ran her fingers through his chest hair. The corners of her mouth pulled down and she pouted her bottom lip.

He never gave her suggestion a thought. 'Sorry, Lisa. I can't. Not yet.' He squeezed her shoulder and kissed her forehead.

'Why not?' She frowned.

'I don't want to rush things between us. Things are fine the way they are, aren't they?'

She pushed him away, stared at him and challenged him further, 'Please, Bill, we've been seeing each other for over a year. I wouldn't say that's rushing things. I've been patient. I'm beginning to think you don't want us to be together, not properly anyway.'

He stroked her cheek. 'Soon; I promise.'

'I love you, Bill.'

His facial expression turned to one of surprise.

An uncomfortable silence followed.

'Oh, just go. Get out!'

Without another word, he got dressed, collected his belongings, left her apartment, and closed the door gently behind him.

She sat on the edge of her bed, naked. She refused to chase after him or shed a tear.

He was not at the following Sunday's walking group. She did not see or hear from him; no telephone calls; no more flowers or poetry. But the more she tried to put him to the back of her mind, the more she thought about him; even more so when she tossed and turned in bed at night.

A few weeks passed. She had got used to him not being in her life when there was a familiar knock on her door. She answered.

He stood in her doorway with a single red rose held out in his hand. He was the last person she had expected to see. 'I've missed you,' he said and then smiled.

'Have you indeed?' She was unsure if she should hug him or slam the door in his face. Her blank facial expression did not give away how she felt inside.

'Yes, I have.' He looked like a schoolboy who waited outside the headmaster's office to be reprimanded.

She stood aside and gestured for him to enter. She closed the door behind him and leant against the door. 'You hurt me, Bill. I deserve better. You disappeared and I didn't hear from you. Where the hell have you been? You only needed to say if you needed space.'

He bowed his head. He had no rational explanation to give.

She took the rose from his hand and helped him take off his jacket.

He smiled as he crouched to take off his shoes.

She had missed him and succumbed to his charm. She held out her hand, led him into the bedroom and placed the rose at the foot of the bed.

They sat for a while on the edge of the bed, in a comfortable silence, and held hands.

A passion burned in his eyes as he turned his head to look at her, but he waited for her to make the first move.

She could not resist him.

They made love and afterwards they laid in each other's arms; their exhausted, perspiring bodies close.

Another comfortable silence followed.

'I've missed you so much these last few weeks. I've not been able to get you out of my mind.' He held her face and kissed her lips. 'I want you to know, I love you too.' He looked into her eyes. 'But my life's complicated.'

She held him closer and felt his slow, strong heartbeat pulsate against her own. Thankful he had come back to her, she decided to take the relationship at his pace and would not put any more pressure on him.

'I'd like to stay with you tonight.' He kissed her forehead. 'If you'd still like me to?'

She nodded and then smiled.

They talked for hours. She updated him with the local gossip; her main source was the bed and breakfast. He told her he had been busy at work.

Dusk arrived. The time had flown. She closed her eyes but did not sleep.

He slipped out of bed, picked up his trousers from the floor, reached into one of the pockets for his mobile and tiptoed towards the bathroom.

She kept still and listened.

He slurred his words as though he were drunk, 'Listen, darling, I'm not going to make it home tonight. I've had one too many and can't drive. I'm going to crash at Gavin's. Yes, I know, darling, I'm sorry. I'll get back as soon as I can in the morning. Will do. Yes. Take care. I love you, too.'

His intended whisper was not quite a whisper, and she had heard every word. Her head spun. She could not think straight. A mixture of theories troubled her. Was he married? Did he already have a girlfriend or was the person on the other end of the line a close family member?

He turned off the bathroom light and crept back into bed.

With her eyes still closed, she stayed still and tried to keep calm. But she felt sick, and her heart pounded against her ribs.

He stroked her face and whispered in her ear, 'I love you, Lisa.'

She had wanted his words to be true. She moved away from him, sat up, slid her feet into her slippers and got out of bed. She made her way towards the door, grabbed her dressing gown from the hook, wrapped it around her and stropped out of the room.

Wide-eyed, he sat up. 'Is everything okay?' he called after her.

She had not wanted to get angry. She had wanted to walk away from the situation and say nothing. 'I'm not tired any more. I need a drink.'

He followed her into the kitchen with an aura of guilt and horror combined.

She sat on her usual chair with her back to him.

'You heard me in the bathroom, didn't you?' He gulped. 'We need to talk. I need to explain. It's not what it seems.'

She had been down that unfaithful road before and would not allow history to repeat itself. 'You don't need to explain anything to me. It is what it is. You just need to get your belongings and go.' She could not look at him.

'I'm, *so*, sorry, Lisa. I should've told you when we first met. You and I were never supposed to happen. I thought we'd just be friends.' His eyes welled up. 'I'm married. My wife's wheelchair bound; not that that's a good enough excuse. She's in that chair because she was in a car crash; a crash I was in too; a crash I caused. I'd been drink-driving.'

She gaped as she turned her head to look at him. 'That's awful.' She stood up, leant over the backrest of another chair, and listened.

'I was young and foolish. Gillian was my girlfriend at the time. One night we'd had an argument in the pub. She stormed out and I went after her in my car. She didn't want to get in because I'd been drinking.' Tears flowed down his cheeks. 'I jumped out of the car and tried to drag her into the car. She eventually got in, but we continued to argue. I got more and more angry and drove faster until I lost control and hit a tree. The rest is history.' He paused. It was obvious he was still racked with guilt. He took deep breaths, calmed himself and continued, 'I can't even remember what we were arguing about. No doubt it was something petty. I got out of the car without so much as a scratch. She was seriously hurt, and it was all my fault. I spent every waking hour with her until she came out of hospital. I proposed to her while she was laid in a hospital bed. I gave her my word I'd look after her forever. I owed her that much.' His eyes were red, and his face was blotchy.

'Oh, my goodness, Bill. You should've told me earlier. We could've just been friends. We shouldn't have allowed our relationship to go this far. If I'd known, I wouldn't have come on so strong with you.' She paused and then nodded. 'Everything makes sense, now. Why you wanted to take things slowly. Why I went for long periods of time without seeing you. Why I've never met any of your friends or family. Why I wasn't allowed to contact you. I feel such a fool. All the signs were there, staring me right in the face.'

He wiped away his tears with the back of his hand. 'Don't you see, Lisa?' He placed his hand on his chest and exhaled audibly.

She shrugged and shook her head. 'See what?'

'I love you. I can't help the way I feel. I want to be with you.'

She took a deep breath as her heart and head battled. 'Don't you see, Bill?' She smiled, a remorseful smile. 'We can't be together, no matter how much we love each other. It wouldn't be fair on Gillian or me. I don't want to be your mistress, your bit on the side. You can't break your promise to your wife either; she needs you.'

'It's not fair. I made one, stupid, mistake when I was young and now, I've got to pay for it for the rest of my life. I don't even love her. I don't think I ever loved her. I pity her.' He clenched his fist against his chest. 'It's eating away at me inside.'

She found it hard to believe what she had heard. 'Imagine how your wife feels. It's not fair on her either. I won't allow you to leave her for me. I wish you'd told me sooner and then it wouldn't have had to come to this. I'd have left you alone, no matter how strong my feelings were.'

'Please, Lisa, we can work it out.' He got down on his knees. 'We have to work it out.'

'I'm going to go back to bed knowing your friendship is still important to me. You can stay tonight, if you want, but you must leave in the morning and go back to your wife.' She was adamant and she would not change her mind.

Nothing more was said. The sadness on their faces said it all. She took off her dressing gown and slippers and got back into bed. He got in beside her, put his arm around her and held her close.

The streetlight outside her bedroom window shone through her curtains. Small black shadows swayed at the foot of her bed. Too exhausted to care, she closed her eyes and drifted off to sleep.

The ticking clock, and the rain as it tapped against the windowpane, interrupted the silence.

Her soul hovered over her bed, a couple of inches beneath the ceiling. She was unsure how or why she did it. The sensation was like floating on water.

She looked down. Bill was no longer cuddled up to her. They slept soundly and looked right together.

An enormous house spider crawled along the duvet, down the side and took refuge beneath her bed.

The bedroom door opened slowly. Small black shadows drifted in through the doorway.

She returned her attention to Bill and watched him as he slept.

The bedroom door opened wider. A large black shadow entered. It appeared not to see her as she hovered above. It floated towards the bed, looked over her body and leant forward until its face was close to hers.

She watched it further.

It straightened up, moved round to Bill's side of the bed, leant forward until its face was close to his and turned its head to look up at her.

She tipped her head to one side.

It copied.

She slowly shook her head as she did not want it to hurt him.

It straightened up, moved away from him, and faded away.

The alarm clock woke her the following morning. The beeping sound had always irritated her. She reached across and turned it off.

Bill did not stir.

She sat on the edge of the bed, stretched out her arms and then shuffled towards the kitchen. She opened the refrigerator door; its light dazzled her. She squinted through one eye as she looked for the orange juice.

He woke, turned over and discovered she had already risen. He found her in the kitchen. 'Morning, Lisa. How are you this morning? Did you sleep well?'

Unsure as to why it was called beauty sleep when she felt more like a troll, she said, 'Morning. On and off. Will you do me a massive favour before you go?'

'Yes,' he said without a second thought. 'Anything.'

'I think I saw a massive spider under the bed. Will you check for me?' She grimaced.

He went back into the bedroom, got down on his hands and knees, lifted the duvet and looked underneath the bed. 'I can't see it.' He checked again and gasped. 'Oh, wait, I think it's up there in the corner.'

She plugged in the vacuum cleaner.

'Wow, he's a big one. Shall we put him outside?' he said.

She handed him the nozzle and flicked on the socket switch. 'No, kill it. I don't want that damn thing coming back in.' She switched on the vacuum.

He laid on his back on the floor and moved into a better position. The spider had heard the vacuum's noise and tried to make a run for it. 'Got it,' he said as he sucked the spider up the nozzle.

'Thank you.' She breathed a sigh of relief and flicked off the switch. 'I hate spiders. Can I make you breakfast as a reward?'

'No thanks.' He picked up his clothes from the floor and shook them. 'I'd better get going. I don't want to prolong this agony any longer.'

Her heart sank, but deep down, she knew it was for the best. She reached out and stroked his cheek. 'Okay.'

'Unless you've changed your mind.' He smiled, yet his eyes welled up.

'No, I haven't changed my mind and I won't be doing either.' She paused. 'Look after Gillian.'

'I still love you,' he said as he got dressed.

'I know, but we can still be friends though, right?'

He nodded and smiled half-heartedly. 'I'd love a hug before I go.'

They made their way towards the door and hugged. Neither of them wanted the moment to end.

'Go.' She pushed him away. 'Before you make me cry.' She watched him put on his shoes and jacket.

'Goodbye, Lisa.' He put up his hand to wave but didn't. 'Take care of yourself.'

She put up her hand to wave but didn't.

He opened the door, left, and closed it gently behind him.

'Goodbye, Bill,' she said. 'I love you, too.' She sighed.

Not in the mood for work, she had to set off thirty minutes later. She finished her juice, put the glass in the sink and made her way into the bathroom.

She turned on the shower and while she waited for the water to run warm, she brushed her teeth.

The mirror above the washbasin had started to steam up. As she wiped it with her palm, she saw the black shadow behind her. She turned round quickly to check, but there was nothing there. She wiped the mirror again with a facecloth and stared at her reflection. A face of someone she barely recognised looked back at her with a pale complexion, sunken cheeks, and darkened sockets around dilated eyes. Her reflection scared her; made the hairs on the back of her neck stand on end. She looked away.

She got undressed, stood beneath the shower, and felt the water flow through her hair, down her face and over her body.

For the first time since she had moved into the apartment, she felt empty and alone.

Chapter Eight

Home Sweet Home

As Lisa pulled up outside the driving test centre again, she felt more confident and less nervous than she had expected. Two other learner cars pulled up at the same time. Both drivers looked young. One of them did not look old enough to be behind the wheel of a car.

Her test was one of the first that day; although, thank goodness, it was after the school run and rush hour.

The examiner was a friendly older lady and was not scary like the horror stories she had heard from other peoples' experiences.

Lisa imagined Stuart was sat in the back of the car and his voice guided her through any given instruction from the examiner. Throughout the test, she exaggerated her head movements when she checked her mirrors and managed not to bounce off any kerbs or hit any stationary objects.

At the end of the test, the examiner put her clipboard down on to her lap and looked over her spectacles at Lisa. 'Congratulations, I'm pleased to tell you, you've passed your practical driving test.' She put her hand out and shook Lisa's hand.

'Wow, I can't quite believe it.' Lisa let out a little screech. 'Thank you so much.' She felt the test had gone well but because the examiner's facial expression was serious, she had expected to hear she had failed.

The examiner smiled as she filled out the necessary paperwork and handed it to Lisa. 'Excellent driving.

Only a couple of minors. I hope you enjoy the rest of your day.'

'Thank you.'

Stuart, who had waited outside the test centre on an old wooden bench, got to his feet when he saw her pull up.

When she saw him, she leapt out of the car, and ran across to him. 'I've passed.' She raised her eyebrows, grinned, and then kissed him on his cheek. 'I can't believe it.'

The examiner had followed. She handed him the car key.

Taken by surprise, he had never received such gratitude. 'Fantastic, Lisa. I knew you could do it.' Before she had spoken, he had worked out the outcome from her excitement. 'I think you need to calm down before you get back behind the wheel. I'll drive you back to your apartment.'

'Thanks, Stuart. I couldn't have done it without you.' She walked back to the car and waited for him while he chatted with the examiner. She leant against the car door and tried to lip-read what they were saying, but to no avail as they were quite a distance away.

He shook the examiner's hand and strolled back towards the car.

Lisa and he talked, and laughed, as he drove her back to her apartment.

She had booked the day off work. What followed her test could have had two possible outcomes: if she failed, she would have wallowed in self-pity while she ate chocolate and watched rubbish on daytime television, or if she passed, she would test drive a few cars she had researched on the internet.

Several cars and a couple of hours later, she decided to go to the Red Squirrel for a late lunch before she made a final decision on which car she would buy. She never usually went during the week, but thought she deserved a treat.

The young barman, who looked fresh out of college and of casual appearance, lacked any enthusiasm. 'What can I get you?'

Not tempted by her usual large glass of red wine, she fancied a nutritional drink instead and she planned to buy a car later, so alcohol was not a good idea. 'I'll have an orange juice, please.'

'Can I order you any food?' He picked at a noticeable scabby spot on the centre of his chin.

If she had not been famished that could have put her off. 'Yes, I'll have a cheese and ham toasty with a side order of chips, please.' It was the first food which came to mind and which her body seemed to crave.

'Any garlic bread to go with your order?' He sounded like he read from a script and would have preferred to be anywhere else.

She wondered how many times he had said that since his shift had started. She feigned a smile before she said, 'No, thank you.'

He tore off the sheet from his order pad and passed it to a colleague who was sat on a stool behind the bar. She appeared as enthusiastic as him. Lisa wondered why she had not noticed the barmaid before as she was covered in tattoos and piercings, not the usual look for the Red Squirrel.

He poured the orange juice into a glass and placed it on the bar. 'That'll be six pounds and seventy-five pence. I'll give you a shout when your food's ready.'

She feigned another smile and handed him a ten-pound note.

'Three pounds and twenty-five pence change.' He smiled at her and continued until she looked away.

Be his smile a sarcastic one or not, she was happy she had changed his mood. She put her change in her purse, zipped it up, picked up her drink and turned round to look for a seat.

Behind her sat Bill and Gillian. She was in a wheelchair with her back to Lisa. He looked across and smiled. He looked well and happy. Lisa had not seen him for weeks. She felt butterflies in the pit of her stomach. She had to decide: should she go across and say hello or ignore him and go and sit somewhere else?

She decided to say hello. She walked across and stood beside the wheelchair, so Gillian could see her. She smiled at Gillian, but she was only really interested in Bill. Her eyes lit up. 'Hi, Bill. How are you? Haven't seen you for ages. Hope you're keeping well.' She wanted to hug and kiss him.

'Hi.' He stayed composed as he looked at Gillian. 'Gillian, this is Lisa.' He gestured.

Lisa felt awkward. 'Hi, Gillian.' She was hesitant. Should she try to shake Gillian's hand?

Gillian lifted her hand and held it out to Lisa. 'Hi, Lisa.' She looked at Bill. 'How do you two know each other?'

'From that walking group I used to go to,' he said quickly.

'Oh, that's nice.' Gillian appeared oblivious to her husband's once infidelity.

An awkward silence followed.

Lisa realised how much she had missed him, if only as a friend. 'I've not seen you there for a while,' she said. 'Will you not be going to the group again?'

He stared down at the table. 'I've been busy with work and looking after Gillian,' he said, a stereotypical answer.

'Also, there was a woman at the group who got on his nerves. She'd become a bit of a nuisance,' Gillian said.

'Oh.' Lisa felt a lump in her throat and gulped. 'I'm sorry to hear that. I think I might know who you mean.' She held back her tears as she looked at Gillian more closely. Gillian was more attractive than she had imagined. She had shiny long curly hair, big eyes with long lashes, kept herself well-groomed and did not appear at all dependent on him. Lisa looked away before Gillian caught her staring.

He alternated his attention between Gillian and Lisa as he bit into his lip, while Gillian looked out of the window.

The atmosphere became tenser by the second.

The barman looked across at Lisa. 'Your toasty and chips are ready.' He placed the plate on the bar.

'Wow, that was quick. Well, it was good to see you, Bill, and lovely to meet you, Gillian. I'll leave you both to it. Enjoy the rest of your day.' She felt relieved of the excuse to walk away. She made her way towards the furthest table from them.

'Yes, good to see you too,' he said, as an afterthought.

She put down her drink, walked back to the bar and collected her food.

'Knives and forks are over there.' The barman pointed across at the cutlery trolley.

'Thanks,' she said; although, she already knew where the trolley was.

As she walked back to her table, past Gillian, and Bill, she overheard part of their conversation.

'Lisa seems like a pleasant girl,' Gillian said.

'She's okay,' he said, in a matter-of-fact manner. As he took a mouthful of beer, he wondered if she had wanted a reaction from him. Did she already know about them? Was it a test?

Lisa picked up the vinegar bottle and squirted it over her chips. She thought about Bill as she nibbled on them. She still loved him and hoped, with time, the feeling would fade. She needed to keep herself busy and focus on more important matters. She thought about the cars she had test driven. But she had already made her mind up before she walked into the pub. She had wanted to give herself a bit more time to make sure she did not change her mind.

Bill stood up and made his way towards the men's toilet.

She tried not to look at him; succeeded when he went in but forgot to make the effort when he came out. He smiled at her. If he expected a smile in return, he would be disappointed. She looked through him, like he was not there.

Bill put on his jacket and wheeled Gillian out of the pub.

Lisa felt saddened and relieved at the same time.

She felt bloated after she had finished her lunch and drink. She stood up, put on her jacket, picked up her handbag and put the strap across her shoulder. She picked up her glass, plate, and cutlery, walked to the bar and placed them on top. 'Thank you.' She smiled at both bar staff in turn. They were the only two people left in the pub, and they looked weary.

'You're welcome,' the barman said as he looked at his watch.

*

Unable to believe she had bought her first car – a little hatchback – she repeatedly looked down at it from her apartment window.

Still full after lunch, she managed a bit of fruit for dinner before she decided to have a bubble bath.

As she started to run the hot water, her landline rang; it was loud, persistent, and difficult to ignore. Unsure of who it might be, she picked up the handset. 'Hello.'

'Hi, Lisa.' It was Bill; his tone confident; his memory short. 'How are you?'

Unable to believe his cheek, she composed herself. Part of her wanted to tell him where to go while the other part decided to be polite. 'I'm fine, thank you, Bill. What can I do for you?'

'I need to see you.' His words were hurried and the desperation in his voice was clear.

'You saw me earlier.' She found it hard to stay polite. 'Why do you need to see me again?' she snapped.

'To tell you how sorry I am, and that I miss you.'

'Apology accepted. But we *both* need to move on.' Surprised by her assertiveness, she continued, 'I've got to go. I'm running a bath and I don't want it to overflow.'

'Please, I need to see you.' He must have known his persistence would not work.

'I don't think that's a good idea, do you?' Of course, she wanted to see him, to hold him, to kiss him, but she would not tell him that.

'I need to explain to your face, Lisa. To tell you how sorry I am about the way I behaved in the pub.' He sniffled.

'Really, there's no need. I understand. You take care of yourself, Bill, and take care of that lovely wife of yours.' Before he had chance to say anything else, she put the handset down and then sighed.

She grabbed her hairbrush, tied up her hair and made her way back towards the bathroom.

The landline rang again. She ignored it and instead watched the bubbles as they multiplied and rose in the bath water. The landline rang off and then at once started again. She turned off the hot water, answered the telephone one last time and then she would leave it off the hook.

'Is that you, Lisa?' The woman's voice sounded panicked.

'Susan, is that you?' Lisa was surprised to hear from her sister as she had not seen or heard from her for a while. 'Whatever's the matter?'

'I've been trying to ring you,' Susan snapped. 'Your phone's always engaged or ringing out.' She paused. 'Mum's had a bad fall down the stairs.'

'Is she going to be, okay?' Lisa, who was always the last to know or left out of the loop altogether when it came to family matters, said.

'She keeps asking to see you, Lisa.'

'Okay.' Lisa raised her eyebrows. 'I'll grab some things and I'll be there as soon as I can.' Although the timing was not right, she had wanted to tell someone her good news all day. 'I'm so excited, Susan. I passed my driving test today and bought my first car.'

'Wow, well done,' Susan tried to sound happy. 'Congratulations. I'll see you soon.'

'Yes, I'll meet you at Mum and Dad's house.'

Susan hung up.

Lisa moved the handset from her ear, tilted her head to one side, and looked at it. Had Susan heard the rendezvous?

Lisa had always known she would have to go back home one day, and it had been a long time since she had seen any of the family. Unsure of how long she would need to stay, she packed a case for several days.

En route, she drove to Woodhayes Bed and Breakfast to update them on what had happened; gave them the good news before the bad. As usual, they understood. She had holiday left to take anyway.

She had no experience of driving on the motorway. She had researched books and watched pointers on the internet but had not expected to be on the motorway so soon and had wanted to have a few lessons with Stuart first.

She stayed in the left-hand lane most of the way; tried to relax but her shoulders were as stiff as an ironing board. The motorway seemed to go on forever but at least the journey was problem free with no traffic jams. It was not long before she got back on to a minor road again.

As she got closer to her old family home, she glanced out of the side windows; noted not much had changed and recognised some of the faces.

She knew the journey was almost over when she drove past Beechwood Park. She parked further up the road from her mum and dad's house, got out of her car, locked the doors, and left her case in the boot.

It felt strange to be back; everything seemed smaller than she remembered. As she made her way towards the house, she dawdled and took in her surroundings.

She knocked on the front door, entered before anyone had chance to answer and was greeted by Susan with a hug.

'It's so good to see you. You look well.' Susan appeared overwhelmed, surprised almost; like she had not expected Lisa to turn up.

'It's good to see you, too. It's been too long.' Lisa looked around to check if anyone else was there. 'Is Karl not with you?'

'No. He's busy with work.' Susan looked down at the floor.

'Where's Dad?' Lisa said through clenched teeth. 'Is he at the hospital with Mum?'

Susan pointed towards the kitchen. 'He's in there, opening a tin of beans for his supper.' She pretended to retch. 'He said he's going to eat them straight out of the can because he can't be bothered to warm them up first and because the wife isn't about to clean up after him.' She rolled her eyes.

'How is he though? Is he coping?' Lisa pretended she cared.

'No idea. You tell me. He's still the same as he always was; a loveable old rogue.' Susan smiled.

Lisa smiled.

They both laughed.

The kitchen door opened. John walked through into the living room. He had not changed much over the years: older, grumpier, and more rotund around his middle.

The house had not changed, like time had stood still. The same pictures hung in the same places and the place still needed to be decorated.

Lisa walked past him and into the kitchen. She looked around and noted he had not bothered to wash-up or put any rubbish into the bin. She opened the bin lid. The bin was already full. She remembered where Elizabeth kept the bin liners, opened the drawer, and got one out.

As the back yard security light came on and illuminated the garden, she remembered how the light used to come on and scare the local cats. She pulled the full liner out of the bin, tied a double knot in the top and looked up at the lawn which still appeared to be in pristine condition. She put the bag on the kitchen floor, moved closer to the window to get a better look and squinted. She was not mistaken. A black shadow hovered, horizontally, about six inches over the lawn.

It moved to an upright position, turned to face her, and then appeared to sit down, cross-legged.

She felt an urge to go outside, like something pulled her towards the back door. She put her hand out to turn the key.

'How long are you going to be staying?' John said as he stood in the doorway. 'I'm asking because there's something I want to watch on the telly.' He tapped his fingers against the doorframe.

She looked out of the window again. The security light had gone off and she could no longer see the black shadow. Unsure if it was still there, she turned round and said, 'Anyway, how are you, Dad? It's been a while. How's Mum? Have you been up to the hospital to see her yet?' She waited for a rude response.

However, he did not answer and instead, he looked at her with a blank facial expression.

Susan, who was stood behind him, rolled her eyes and shook her head.

Lisa, who had long since hardened to his lack of paternal emotions, said, 'Don't worry, I'm not staying. I'm going to book myself into the bed and breakfast down the road. I'm only here to see Mum, anyway.'

Without a word or any show of concern, he turned round, made his way back into the living room, flopped into his chair and aimed the remote control at the television. It was the same television they had watched when they were little; a miracle it had not worn out.

Lisa and Susan made their way out through the front door and closed it behind them.

Lisa turned to Susan and said, 'I'll go and book myself into Valley View Bed and Breakfast. Fingers crossed they'll have a room available for me. I don't think I'd be welcome, or that it'd be a barrel of laughs, if I slept on Mum and Dad's sofa, do you?'

Susan followed Lisa to her car. The years had not been kind to her. She had not aged well; permanent worry lines ran across her forehead. 'I'll come with you and then we can get straight off to the hospital.' She paused, looked Lisa up and down. 'It's good to see you. You seem different somehow.'

Lisa got into the driver's seat and pulled her seat belt across her. She thought it strange to have Susan sat beside her. As she put the key in the ignition, she turned her head to look at Susan. 'How did Mum manage to fall?'

Susan shook her head. 'I don't know.' She shrugged. 'I know as much as you. We'll ask her when we get to the hospital.'

'Do you think she'll tell us the truth this time? She's protected that man for long enough.' Lisa turned the key and drove towards Valley View. The rest of the journey was quiet; both were deep in thought.

Lisa managed to book the last single room at the bed and breakfast. Not as comfortable as home, but it was clean and cosy. She got her case from the boot and carried it up to her room while Susan waited in the car.

With a spring still in her step, she got back into her car. 'Right, let's get up to the hospital. I'll unpack later.'

At the start of the journey there was an uncomfortable silence until Susan snapped out of her trance, turned her head to look at Lisa and said, 'How's Bill?'

'Yes, he's good. So's his wife.' Lisa glanced at Susan to gauge her reaction.

'What? He's married? Oh. My. God.' Susan gaped.

'Yes, Gillian seems nice.'

Whatever Susan had thought about before was forgotten. 'What! You've met her?'

156

Lisa stopped at a red traffic light. No one waited at the crossing but a young boy, who had obviously pressed the button, ran along the path. He stopped, checked behind him, stuck out his tongue and put up his index and middle fingers. She sniggered. 'Indeed, I have. By accident, though. They were sat together in my local pub earlier today.'

'So, you found out he's married today?'

'No, I found out a while ago. Today was the first time I'd seen his wife at all and him in a while.' Lisa took a deep breath and sighed. She did not want to talk about them anymore. 'It was difficult seeing them together, but I got through it.'

Susan's questions continued, 'You must have been mortified. How did you find out?'

Lisa wished she had not brought up the subject but until she had answered all Susan's questions, she knew there would be no end to the matter. 'He was at mine. I heard him on the phone with her. The funny thing was it was the only night he stayed all night at mine.' She paused. 'When I asked him, though, he did tell me everything.'

The traffic light turned green. She drove on but found it difficult to concentrate. Her mind wandered back to Bill. She pictured how happy he and Gillian had appeared as they sat together in the pub. Her memories confirmed she had made the right decision.

The cheeky, little, button pusher was further along the road. She beeped twice on her car horn at him. He turned his head to look. She stuck out her tongue and waved.

'Didn't you kick off? You'd been seeing him for months,' Susan said.

Lisa glanced sideways at Susan. 'I told him we should just be friends.' She paused. 'I do understand why he lied to me you know.'

Susan wriggled back on her seat, straightened up and folded her arms. 'You always were the calmer one of us. I'd have kicked his arse into next week.' She tittered.

The questions stopped.

They reached the outer ring road. The hospital was a short distance away.

Not confident enough to park in the hospital's busy car park, Lisa parked on a nearby side road instead.

She reached across Susan and got her purse from the glove compartment. They got out of the car, locked it, and made their way towards the hospital. Lisa wished she had put on a thicker jumper. Once they were inside the hospital grounds, they followed the signs for *reception*.

A young man greeted them, with a smile, from behind his computer. He had been in the warmth for some time and had rosy cheeks.

Lisa stayed quiet and let Susan ask the question, 'Could you tell us which ward Elizabeth Parkins is on, please?'

He pressed several keys on his keyboard and studied his computer screen. He looked up and said, 'Yes, Mrs Parkins is on ward A3: the burns ward.'

Susan frowned, glanced at Lisa, and then turned her attention back to the young man. She took a deep breath and looked at him through squinted eyes. 'The burns ward. Are you sure? Do you have the right Elizabeth Parkins?'

He pressed the same keys on his keyboard and checked his screen again. 'Yes, there's only been one Elizabeth Parkins admitted.'

Lisa, who did not want to interfere, looked down at her shoes. She waited on Susan's decision on what they should do next.

Susan was a little flushed, which could have been because the hospital was too warm, or she was embarrassed. 'Okay, thank you.' Unsure what to do next, she waited a moment before she turned round and pointed at the *ward A3* sign.

Lisa followed her and the signs. As they walked past the gift shop, she glanced at the buckets filled with bunches of flowers. She did not have time to stop because Susan rushed ahead. She would call back later.

'I don't understand.' Susan stopped and turned to look at Lisa. 'How did Mum manage to burn herself while she was falling down the stairs?'

Lisa shrugged. 'Ward A3 is to the right.' She gestured.

A few corridors and a trip in a lift later, they were greeted by a nurse as they entered the ward: a young woman with a strong Eastern European accent. 'Ladies, could I ask you both to use the hand sanitizer before you enter?' She pointed at a unit on the wall behind them, beside the entrance's swinging doors.

Neither of them had noticed the hand sanitizer sign as they entered. Their minds were on a more pressing matter. They did as they were asked, walked back to the unit, and pushed the button. The unit squirted a small amount of gel on to their palms. They rubbed the gel into their hands and walked towards the nurses' station.

The same nurse stepped out in front of them again. 'How can I help you, ladies?'

'We're here to visit our mother, Elizabeth Parkins,' Lisa said.

The nurse, whose mascara had smudged beneath her eyes, must have worked a long shift because her patience appeared to have dwindled. 'You are aware visiting hours are over?' She tried to keep her professionalism, but she appeared flustered. 'The hours are clearly stated on the door.'

Lisa checked what the time was on her watch. She had not realised how late it was. Her day off work had turned out more eventful than she had planned. 'No, I'm sorry, we hadn't realised,' she said quietly. She hoped she had not had a wasted journey. 'I've travelled a long way to visit my mum, though. Could we pop in to say a quick hello? We won't be long or cause a disturbance.'

The nurse sighed. 'Okay, but only for a short while. In future you stick to the visiting hours, please. Follow me. I will show you to her bed.'

They reached a side room with four beds. The nurse pointed across at Elizabeth who was laid beside the window. The room was quiet. One of the other patients was already asleep; one read a book; another watched television with their headphones on.

'Thank you,' Susan said. 'It's much appreciated.' She smiled.

'Yes, thank you,' Lisa whispered. She smiled and followed Susan.

They approached their mother cautiously as they did not want to make her jump.

Elizabeth, who looked out through the window, had seen their reflections. She turned her head and smiled, but their serious facial expressions made her burst into tears.

They hurried to either side of her, put their arms around her and hugged her.

'Ow.' Elizabeth winced.

Both recoiled.

'Oops, sorry, Mum,' Susan said.

Elizabeth pulled her clinging nightie away from her chest.

Lisa picked up two chairs from the stack underneath the window and placed them beside the bed.

They tried to keep their conversation as quiet as possible, but the whispers often got louder.

'Mum, what's happened? How are you?' Susan said. She scraped her chair along the floor to get closer to Elizabeth and then placed her hand over Elizabeth's hand.

'I've been better.' Elizabeth wiped her eyes with the back of her hand. 'I've been my usual clumsy self and fallen down the stairs.'

'Then why are you in the burns ward, Mum?' Lisa could see how upset her mum was, but she felt annoyed and wanted her mum to admit what a bully John was. 'What really happened? Cut the bullshit and be honest. I can see the burn on your chest.'

An elderly lady, in the next bed, looked across at them and frowned. Disgusted by Lisa's language, she turned her back on them.

Lisa stood up and pulled the curtain along.

'I spilt a pan of boiling water down myself.' Elizabeth held back her tears. 'I get clumsier as I get older.'

Susan turned her head to look at Lisa and frowned. 'Jesus, back off a bit, will you. Can't you see Mum's in agony?'

'Back off? Are you for real?' Lisa snapped. She looked at Elizabeth again. 'How on earth did you burn your chest? Were you carrying the pan on your head?'

Susan sat back on her chair, sighed, and continued to frown.

The nurse stood at the foot of the bed. Her left eyebrow raised as she looked at Lisa and then at Susan. 'Can you, ladies, keep the noise down? You are disturbing the other patients. I am going to have to ask you to leave soon and ask you to come back tomorrow during visiting hours; where I hope you will act in a more considerate manner.' She left to talk to the lady in the next bed.

Lisa leant forward and whispered to Elizabeth, 'I called in to see Dad before we came here to visit you. He made it obvious he couldn't wait to see the back of me. I haven't seen him for ages, and he couldn't even muster a hello or how are you?' She had been pulled from her new life back to the one she had escaped from, and she wanted answers. 'You've got to stop protecting that man, Mum. He's a complete arsehole. The man's got no soul.'

'You don't know it was dad,' Susan said. She had always lived with her head buried in the sand; preferred to hide away from what stared her in the face. 'Why do you always have to be so nasty?'

Lisa stayed calm and did not look at Susan. 'Yes, it was, and you know it.' She moved closer to Elizabeth and whispered, 'Mum, what have you told the doctors and nurses?' Then she looked her straight in the eye.

'That I spilt a pan of boiling water down myself.' Elizabeth pursed her dry lips which made them look white.

Lisa knew Elizabeth lied. 'Do they believe you?'

'Yes, I think so or they'd have called the police, wouldn't they?' Tears started to roll down Elizabeth's cheeks. 'Please, Lisa, I don't want any more trouble.'

Lisa put her hand over Elizabeth's. 'Mum, please, I'm begging you; tell me what really happened?'

Susan, who no longer frowned, remained quiet and bit into her bottom lip. She realised there was more to what Elizabeth had said and she also wanted to know the truth.

Lisa did not blink as she looked Elizabeth in the eye. 'I can't and won't let this go, Mum. I need to know; so, you might as well tell me.'

Elizabeth's hand shook. 'What will you do?' She looked down at it.

Lisa did not answer.

'All right.' Elizabeth shook her head, as though she tried to stop herself. 'Your father threw the water at me.'

Susan started to sob and at once wiped her tears away with the back of her hand.

Lisa had already known what the answer would be, but the truth had not made her feel any better. 'Accidentally or on purpose?'

After years of mental and physical abuse, Elizabeth was relieved the truth was finally out; a weight lifted from her shoulders. Her shoulders relaxed. 'On purpose.' She sighed. 'All because we didn't have any spare batteries in the house for his precious telly remote. He can never be bothered to get up off his backside and press the buttons on the damn telly himself.'

Lisa felt her heart pulsate against her ribs. She got to her feet, leant forward and kissed Elizabeth's forehead. 'I'm going to ring Grandma and Grandad Buckley and ask them to fly over as soon as they can.'

Elizabeth nodded.

Susan's frown had returned. 'Why? What can they do?'

Amazed by Susan's lack of thought, Lisa was unsure if Susan's remissness was deliberate or if she was not on the same wavelength. 'They could take Mum back to Spain with them; get her away from that monster, even if it's just for a while.'

'He's not always like that, Lisa,' Susan snapped.

'So, you think it's okay for him to scald our mother?' Lisa's scowl should have turned Susan to stone. 'You've got a short and selective memory if you're still putting that man on a pedestal.'

'I have to admit he is getting worse, though,' Elizabeth interrupted. 'If I'm being honest, I don't even love him anymore.'

'No, Mum,' Susan said. 'Everything'll be okay. Things will calm down again and get back to how they used to be.'

'That's exactly what I don't want,' Elizabeth said. 'Please don't make this any harder for me. You know, deep down, what he's really like. You need to come to terms with his behaviour, like I finally have.' She paused. 'Would you do me a favour?'

'Yes, of course, Mum,' Susan said.

'I need to have a quick word with Lisa. Would you mind going to the shop to get me a couple of magazines, please?' She reached across into the bedside cabinet drawer and took a five-pound note from her purse. 'You don't mind, do you?' She held out the note.

Susan's response did not correspond with what she thought. 'Yes, no worries.' She took the note.

Elizabeth watched Susan until she was out of sight.

'I'll go and make that call,' Lisa said.

Elizabeth grabbed Lisa's wrist. 'No, please, wait.'

'Don't try to stop me, Mum. Do you know how much I hate what he's done to us all these years?' Her eyes welled up. 'I hate the way he treats you; you're like his slave.' She took a deep breath. 'I don't care how he treats me anymore; I'm immune to his ways.'

'I'm not going to try to stop you.' Elizabeth let go of Lisa's wrist. 'I just need you to come back tomorrow so I can tell you something when Susan isn't here. We don't have time to talk now because she could be back any minute.'

'Okay, Mum, I will. I'll be back soon once I've spoken to Grandma.' Lisa walked out of the room with her mobile pressed against her ear.

Susan was back at Elizabeth's bedside by the time Lisa had finished her call. Lisa walked round to the other side of the bed, leant forward, and whispered, 'They're going to get a flight tomorrow. I haven't told them everything, though. You need to be the one to do that, Mum.' She nodded and tried to reassure her with a smile.

'Thanks, Lisa.'

The nurse looked across at them.

'I'm going to head back to the bed and breakfast. I'll see you soon,' Lisa said.

'Oh, and congratulations.' Elizabeth smiled. 'I heard you've passed your driving test and bought yourself a car. You kept that quiet.'

'Thanks, Mum.' Lisa winked and then waved. 'We've got a lot of catching-up to do.'

As she drove back, she turned on the radio, turned up the volume and sang along. The return journey to the bed and breakfast seemed shorter.

She parked up the car, locked it, and made her way up to her room.

She took off her make-up, had a quick body wash and cleaned her teeth. When she emptied her case, she realised she had forgotten her pyjamas and would have to sleep in her knickers and a T-shirt or go naked.

Plenty had happened that day and it took her a while to get to sleep. She listened to the sound of a distant train as she drifted off.

Chapter Nine

The Truth

The next morning, Lisa was woken by the telephone on the dressing table. She did not wake straight away as the sound was quieter than her alarm clock at home. She picked up her watch from the bedside table and looked at the time: seven thirty. She had asked reception to give her an alarm call so she could go down for breakfast early. She answered the telephone and then laid back down on the bed for a moment as she felt more tired than usual and nauseous.

A little while later, she sat up, got up and got dressed. She would shower after breakfast. She put a brush through her hair and tied it up with a scrunchy. She picked the dried bits out of her tear ducts and rubbed her eyes.

She was the first guest down for breakfast. A pleasant smell greeted her as she entered the dining area. It was peaceful which allowed her time to reflect. The room was small with a few tables set out. The décor was tasteful and looked expensive. The breakfast spread was impressive; most of the food was sourced locally. She had a bowl of grapefruit, a natural yoghurt, and a full English without black pudding. The food was delicious. Everything had been grilled or boiled. She finished with a glass of fresh orange juice before she made her way back up to her room.

The floorboards creaked as she walked up the stairs and along the landing to her room. She heard faint conversations through other guests' doors.

She closed the door behind her, picked up the remote control and switched on the television so she could catch up with the local news.

While she undressed, she heard a tap turn on and off in the bathroom. She made her way towards the bathroom and as she opened the door cautiously, she expected to see another guest in there, but the room was empty. She looked in the washbasin; the last few drops of water trickled down the plughole. There was a faint odour, like someone had passed through with a cigar; the same smell she had noticed when she moved into her apartment.

She reached up and latched the window handle on to night vent. Outside the door, she flicked on the light switch which triggered the extraction.

As she tried to work out how the shower worked, she felt nauseous again and dashed towards the toilet. She felt hot and clammy as she knelt on the cold tiled floor. She wrapped her arms around the toilet, retched and then vomited. She flushed the toilet and sat down on the floor. The cool breeze from the opened window made her feel a little better. She put her head back, closed her eyes and waited for the nausea to pass.

She felt weak as she got to her feet and took her time as she worked out how to turn on the shower again. She set the water temperature cooler than usual and stepped beneath its flow. She closed her eyes, breathed slowly, and felt the water stream through her hair, down her face and over her body.

She felt refreshed as she turned off the shower and wrapped a towel around herself. She made her way towards the washbasin and put toothpaste on to her toothbrush.

A scary thought came to mind as she stared at herself, wide-eyed, in the heated mirror. When was her last period? She could usually pinpoint to the exact date.

The telephone started to ring. She spat toothpaste into the washbasin, wiped a facecloth over her mouth and went through into the bedroom. She put the television on mute and picked up the handset. 'Hello,' she said.

'Hi, Lisa, it's Susan. Sorry to ring you so early. I wasn't sure if you'd be up yet. I wanted to know what time you planned on visiting Mum today.'

Lisa wondered why Susan had not rung her on her mobile. 'Morning, Susan. No, you're fine. I still get up early every day. You know me. I've never been one to lay in bed. I wasn't going to visit Mum until later today. I've got a few errands I need to run this morning,' she lied and felt bad because Susan sounded sincere.

'Will it be okay if I tag along with you, again, later today? I'm not a big fan of hospitals and I'd prefer to go along with someone else.'

'Yes, no worries.' Lisa wanted to keep the conversation short as she needed to get out of the wet towel and get dressed. 'I'll ring you later. We'll work something out.'

'Okay, thanks, Lisa.'

'See you soon.' Lisa put down the handset.

She turned off the television, sat on the edge of the bed and dried between her toes. As she stood up, she caught sight of her stomach in the dressing table mirror. She turned sideways, pulled her stomach in and out again; repeated a couple more times before she decided her stomach did not look bigger. She placed her hand on her stomach, as though she had some sort of psychic ability and was able to feel if she was pregnant or not and then shook her head. She laughed as she got dressed but soon stopped when she noticed her jeans felt tighter around her waist.

She checked around and made sure she had turned off all the electrical appliances. She put on her shoes and jacket, grabbed her handbag and car keys, and made her way to the hospital.

The journey was horrendous. She felt like she was in a real-life Hazard Perception Test: panicked mums were parked in illegal places and caused obstructions; parents and their children ran around as they tried to get to the school gate on time while commuters made their way to work. She had to stop at every crossing and every traffic light appeared to conspire against her.

She arrived at the hospital in plenty of time for the first visiting hours. She parked on the same side road and walked towards the hospital.

As she made her way towards the ward, she stopped off at the shop and bought Elizabeth a bunch of red carnations and a box of milk chocolates.

Much to her surprise, Grandma and Grandad Buckley had already arrived from Spain and were sat at Elizabeth's bedside. 'Hi, Grandma. Hi, Grandad. How long's it been since I last saw you both?' she said. 'You managed to get here quickly.' She hugged her grandparents, in turn, and kissed them on the cheek. She hugged Elizabeth cautiously and kissed her forehead.

'Yes, we decided to get a flight as soon as we could. We were so worried. Your mum's told us what's happened. To be honest, the news didn't come as a shock to us,' Grandma said. She smiled at Lisa. 'My, Lisa, I have to say you're glowing. Have you got something you need to tell us?'

Lisa tittered. 'No, I don't think so.' She felt her face redden as she got another chair and sat on the opposite side of the bed.

A nurse made her way towards them. Her bedside manner was warmer than the nurse from the previous night. 'Only two to a bedside, I'm afraid; hospital regulations.'

Grandad lost his balance as he got to his feet and grabbed the chair back. 'I'll go and stretch my legs. See if I can find a vase for those beautiful flowers at the same time. I'll leave you three beautiful ladies to have a catch-up.'

'Thank you, Grandad.' Lisa watched him shuffle out of the room. She turned to look at Elizabeth, reached out and held her hand. 'And how are you feeling today, Mum?' Elizabeth seemed happier than she had the night before. In fact, Lisa could not remember the last time she had seen her look so cheerful.

'I'm okay in myself. Still sore though, which goes without saying.'

Lisa smiled and let go of Elizabeth's hand. She made her way round to the other side of the bed, leant forward, put her arms around her grandma and hugged her again. The smell of mothballs and musky perfume greeted her. 'How are, you, and Grandad? I've missed you both.'

Grandma patted Lisa's back. 'We're fine, Lisa. Can't complain. Not getting any younger, though. Anyway, go and sit yourself down. Your mum needs to talk to you.'

Lisa did as she was told. 'What is it?' Her eyes welled up. 'Oh no, Mum. You're not dying, are you?'

Elizabeth adjusted her pillows, made herself comfortable and then leant forward. 'I need you to listen and I need you to understand. I don't want you to get upset or angry or make a scene.'

'Okay, Mum, I'll try. I'm all ears.'

'I'm telling you now, while I can, because John's not here and while I have the courage. I needed you to be here, so I could look you in the eye when I told you. I didn't want to explain over the telephone.'

Grandma got up from her chair, made her way around the bed to Lisa and stood behind her. She placed her hands on Lisa's shoulders and kissed the top of her head.

'I'm sorry, Lisa. I realise I should have told you years ago. I didn't know how, and I was too scared.' Elizabeth looked at her mother, gulped and took a deep breath.

Grandma nodded.

Elizabeth looked Lisa in the eye again. 'I'm going to get straight to the point and say it outright. John *isn't* your real father. Your biological father was one of John's friends. And you look so much like him, and you remind me so much of him. I know he would have been proud of you.'

Lisa remained silent. She knew she should have felt shocked, but the truth was, she didn't. She had always known something was not right in her life. All at once, everything started to make sense. Intrigued, she continued to listen.

Elizabeth spoke quietly as the elderly lady in the next bed might not have been asleep, 'I met him through John. Started to see him at the same time. It was only meant to be a bit of fun. I didn't think it'd turn into anything serious. John and I had only just started seeing each other. Everything happened so fast. John was so intense and serious, and Peter Hurst was such a loveable rogue. He had all the qualities John didn't. I wish I'd met him first. Oh, how I loved him.' Her face lit up as she talked of him. 'When I found out I was pregnant, I was going to finish with John when, unexpectedly, Peter died. John told me Peter had been shot in a bank raid. I never saw him again. I was heartbroken. I couldn't imagine life as a single mum. I decided the easiest choice was to stay with John. I didn't have much choice. I hope you understand, Lisa.'

Lisa understood why it had been difficult for Elizabeth to tell her the truth. 'Peter, my real dad, died in a bank raid? Was he a bank robber or an innocent bystander?' She was not concerned about the answer.

'He was one of the bank robbers. It was strange though because he'd never mentioned that side of his life to me. I thought we knew everything there was to know about each other. As you can imagine, the news came as quite a shock to me. You must understand, Peter was a caring man who'd have gone to any length to help the ones he loved.'

Grandad returned. He knew what the conversation had been about. 'One of the nurses is going to bring a vase across for you, when they find a spare one.'

'My turn to go and stretch my legs. Are you going to be okay, Lisa?' Grandma said.

Lisa did not answer; she was deep in thought.

Grandad flopped down on the chair and sighed.

Elizabeth waited for Lisa's inevitable questions.

'How do you know Peter was my father and not John?' Lisa said.

'Because I hadn't slept with John. When you were born, I had to tell him you were premature.'

'Does John know about you and my real father? Does he know he's not really my father? Does he know his friend is my father?'

'No, I don't think so. To be honest, we never talked about it.' Relieved to finally confess after many years, Elizabeth's shoulders slumped.

'Did Peter know about me?'

'He did, yes, and he was so excited. We'd made plans, which is why I was surprised when John told me Peter had been killed in a bank raid.'

Lisa was unsure if she should laugh or cry. She felt sad about Peter because she had never met him and anger towards John because he had bullied and undermined her all her life.

'I wish you'd told me before, though.' Lisa had a thought. 'Mum, did Peter smoke cigars?'

'Yes, he did. Why do you ask?'

'Oh, just a feeling, that's all. Do you have any photos of him or any newspaper cuttings from when he robbed the bank? I want to know more about him. In fact, I want to know everything about him.'

'The funny thing is, I never saw anything in the newspapers about any bank robbery. I looked for days after, but there was never any mention of it.' Elizabeth paused. 'I think I've still got a photo of him hidden away somewhere. I'll have a look when I get chance and let you have it.' She was pleased Lisa had taken the news so well.

'What are you doing here? I thought you were going to ring me?' Susan said.

'Hi, Susan. I was just passing, so I thought I'd pop in.'

Susan took off her jacket and draped it over the back of Lisa's chair. 'What have I missed?' She looked around.

'Nothing much. Sorry, I'm going to have to get off.' Lisa looked pale and sweaty. 'I'm not feeling well, and I've still got a few errands I need to run.'

'Will I see you again soon?' Elizabeth said.

'Of course, you will. Take care of yourself.' Lisa placed her hand on Elizabeth's shoulder and kissed her cheek. 'I'll come back tonight.' She turned to look at grandad. 'See you soon, Grandad. Give Grandma my love.' She turned to look at Susan. 'I'll ring you later.'

Chapter Ten

John and Elizabeth

John Parkins and Elizabeth Buckley had been in the early stage of their relationship and had met a few months earlier.

He travelled up from Cornwall to visit her whenever he got chance, which was usually after he had finished work on a Friday, until eventually, he visited every weekend.

Train fares were expensive and took up a lot of his hard-earned cash, so he arrived with his rucksack and pitched his tent in the corner of Beechwood Park field. Local lads did the same. No one ever bothered any of them or complained.

John and Elizabeth loved their time in the park together without their parents' prying eyes. In the evenings, she snuck out to meet him in his tent; told her parents she was with friends and would be back late. She always wore too much perfume and make-up, and not enough clothes. Her parents would smile; they remembered what it had felt like to not have a care in the world and your life in front of you.

John and Elizabeth liked to sit beside the river, share a picnic and look up at the stars. He talked about his week at work, and she listened, sometimes. Often, she let her mind wander; daydreamed about meeting a tall handsome stranger who would sweep her off her feet and look after her forever as though she were a princess. John made her feel comfortable, but she was not sure if he was the one, she wanted to spend the rest of her life with.

One evening, he had waited beside the river for her. He had been there for some time and had started to believe she had stood him up because she was usually punctual.

A distinguished-looking gentleman, who smoked a cigar, walked along the path towards the bench beneath the sycamore.

John watched the man. He had seen him there before; sometimes alone; sometimes with others.

The man sat down on the bench and rested the calf of one leg over the knee of his other leg. He saw John look across at him and he waved.

Not used to polite strangers, John hesitated before he waved and nodded once.

The man gestured for John to join him.

Unsure if to join the man or not, John got to his feet; although, he felt he did not have a choice. He brushed grass from his trousers with his hand and made his way towards him.

The man made no attempt to stand as he took a pull on his cigar. He blew the smoke out and said, 'Are you all right, mate? I've not seen you round here before. You look a little lonely. Are you lost?'

John looked at the man's pinstriped suit and tie. He thought it strange for him to be dressed so formal at that time of day and in a park; perhaps he had just finished work, or he was a gangster. 'Just visiting,' he said.

The man uncrossed his legs, leant forward, and held out his hand. 'I'm Peter, Peter Hurst. Hursty to my nearest and dearest. And you are?'

'John Parkins.' He shook Peter's hand. 'But most people call me John.'

Peter tightened his grip. 'Well, John. It's nice to meet you. You're not local to these parts, are you? Your accent's the giveaway.' A spark of energy passed through his hand into John's. 'Anyway, what do you think of our park?'

John pulled his hand away and wiggled his fingers. He dismissed the sensation as a static shock. Unsure as to what Peter wanted with him, he looked at him through narrowed eyes. 'Yes, it's okay.' He nodded. 'Appears to be popular with the locals and always seems busy.'

'Would you like to join us, John, or are you waiting for someone in particular?' Peter closed his eyes as he took a long drag on his cigar and then exhaled through his mouth and nose.

'Thanks, but I'm waiting for my girlfriend.'

Peter nodded once. 'No worries. Anytime, John.' He leant back and re-crossed his legs.

Without a care in the world, Elizabeth walked along the path towards them. She looked around her, stopped to look up at the sky and watched as birds flew from tree to tree.

'Here's Elizabeth now.' John's face lit up as he pointed to her and then made his way towards her. 'Where have you been?' He grabbed her hand and pulled her to hurry her along. 'You're late for goodness' sake.'

Elizabeth frowned. She had not seen him behave that way before; it was not a side of him she liked or wished to see again. 'I'm sorry, all right. I had things to do, and I didn't realise what the time was.'

'Anyway, never mind your excuses.' His behaviour was akin to a petulant child. 'Come and say hello to Peter.'

She yanked her hand from his grip. 'Peter?' She was undecided if she should stay or turn round and go home.

Peter stayed seated and watched John and Elizabeth as they approached.

Although she had never spoken with Peter before, she felt somehow drawn to him. He mesmerised her and the closer she got to him the more her face lit up.

John stood taller. 'Peter, this is Elizabeth,' he said, as though he showed-off his prize-winning dog at Crufts.

'Yes, thank you, John. You've already said.' Peter stood up, threw his cigar on to the ground, stamped on it, and blew out any residual smoke. 'Well, hello, Elizabeth.' He kept eye contact as he leant forward and kissed the back of her hand. 'It's made my day meeting such an attractive young woman.'

Elizabeth blushed. 'Hi, Peter.' She tried to look away but found it impossible; her eyes were magnetized towards his.

Proud he had made a new friend, John stood back; oblivious that Peter flirted with his girlfriend.

'I do believe I've seen you before, Elizabeth.' Peter continued to hold her hand and looked into her eyes, as though he tried to look into her soul. 'Do you live local?'

'Yes, I do.' Her eyes twinkled. 'I don't think I recognise you though. I'm sure I'd remember if I'd seen you before.'

He looked away. 'Why don't you two stay and meet the rest of the group?' He gestured for them to sit.

As she sat down on the middle of the bench, she hoped he would sit beside her, but neither Peter nor John joined her.

Peter continued his conversation with John and appeared to ignore her. 'We usually meet up later, but George must get back home to look after his daughter, Vicky, tonight. She's a beautiful young girl. She's going to break some hearts one day.'

'Do you meet every day? What do you talk about? Is there a reason you meet up here?' John had many questions. 'How many are in the group?'

'We try to meet up every day; although, it's not always possible. We probably meet up here for the same reason as you two; people tend to mind their own business and let you get on with your own thing. And there's not many of us yet; there's me, George Willis, and my old man: Fred. Are you two going to hang round then?'

Elizabeth waited for John to answer.

He shrugged.

'This is George coming now. Handsome chap, isn't he?' Peter laughed. 'His daughter clearly gets her looks from her mother.'

Elizabeth chuckled.

John remained serious.

George carried a large black holdall which looked like it had had plenty of use as it was worn and fell apart in places. He placed the holdall down on the ground carefully, but it still hit the ground with a thud. He put his hand out and introduced himself, 'George Willis.'

John shook his hand. 'John Parkins and this is my girlfriend, Elizabeth Buckley.'

George looked at Elizabeth and smiled. 'Pleased to meet you both. Here for the meeting?' He raised his eyebrows.

'Not sure,' John said. He looked at Elizabeth, who remained quiet.

'Is your old man coming tonight, Peter?' George said.

'He should be. Said he was going to close the shop up early.' Peter looked at John and then at Elizabeth. 'He owns a junk shop in the village and when I say junk that's what I mean. Still the shop keeps him happy and out of mischief.'

Again, Elizabeth chuckled while John remained serious.

George looked at his watch. 'We'll have to make a start. I've got to make tracks soon and get back for Vicky. Elizabeth, John, would you like to join us or spectate today?'

'I'll spectate, thank you,' Elizabeth said.

John scowled; he was not happy with her decision. 'I'll join you, George.'

Undecided if to go home or wait for John, she made her way towards the swing and sat down.

Fred arrived. 'Evening, all.'

Peter did not need to make any introductions. It was obvious Fred was his father as they had similar mannerisms and looked alike.

George started to empty the contents of his holdall. He pulled out a large object which was covered with a towel. He uncovered it and placed the demon-like statue on the ground beneath the pentangle on the sycamore. He handed everyone a rolled-up mat.

In turn, they kissed the top of the statue and knelt back down on their mats.

John, who had heard of similar groups before and thought it harmless to join in, did not ask any questions and followed George's lead.

Elizabeth watched. She thought they were strange and wondered why they played little boys' games.

John glanced across at Elizabeth before he took his turn.

She looked at him with a blank facial expression.

George started to chant. Peter and Fred joined in. John did not join in as he did not know a word of Latin.

George's face looked odd as he stared at John. The colour had drained from his face and his cheeks appeared sunken.

John felt hypnotised, no longer in control, and found he was able to speak Latin fluently as he started to chant.

Five small black shadows appeared and swayed around the statue.

Elizabeth had not noticed as she stared at her feet beneath the swing. It was the flash of light which caught her attention.

'Well, looks like that's it for today,' George said. 'The spirits didn't want to come out and play for long.' He collected the mats and packed the statue into his holdall.

John nodded at George and then stood a while longer as he tried to process what had happened.

Elizabeth watched John as he made his way towards her. 'What was all that about?' she said.

'If you were really interested, you'd have joined us. I'm going to come back tomorrow and meet up with them again.'

She did not respond.

The weeks passed. When he visited at the weekends, he spent more time with the group than he did with Elizabeth.

He decided to move closer and bought a small, terraced house and started to landscape the garden.

During the day, she visited the park as she wanted to bump into Peter. She tried different days and times until she timed her visit perfectly. When she saw him, she questioned if she had made the right decision. But it was too late; Peter had already seen her.

He waved.

'Oh hi, Peter.' She tried to act surprised as she made her way towards him.

'Hi, Elizabeth.' He smirked and then winked. 'So glad you remembered my name. I've not seen you for a while. I see John most nights. What are you doing here? You're not by yourself, are you?'

'Just taking a stroll and getting some fresh air. You know how it is. What about you?' She wrapped strands of hair around her index finger and tucked them behind her ear.

'Just out for a walk and hoping to bump into you. Looks like it's my lucky day.'

She felt herself blush. 'Bump into me? Why on earth would you want to do that?'

'I thought that would have been obvious, Elizabeth.' He leant forward, kissed the back of her hand and then her lips. He stepped back and looked at her face.

Her eyes were still closed, and her lips still pursed. She opened her eyes, looked at him, took a deep breath and kissed him on his lips.

'Wow, I wasn't expecting that,' he said. 'I thought I'd, at least, get a slap across the face.'

She held his face and kissed him again. 'Meet me tonight.' She smiled, nodded, and then kissed him again.

'I'll try, but I've got to go to the meeting first.'

'Why? What are they about?'

'Listen, George is my best buddy and he's wanted to set those prayer meetings up for years; for as long as I can remember. I don't want to let him down.'

'Why? You know they're not normal, right? They're weird.'

'Meet me at the bridge around nine.' He pulled her closer, hugged her and squeezed her bottom.

As they walked off in opposite directions, they peeked at each other over their shoulders'.

Chapter Eleven

The Death of Peter Hurst

During his lunch break, George often rushed home to walk his puppy, Patch, a black Labrador, through the park.

Several weeks into Peter and Elizabeth's affair, George saw them together beside the river. He stopped close by. But the couple were oblivious to him, and an excitable Patch, and only focussed on each other. Still both fully clothed, Peter laid on top of Elizabeth and kissed her passionately.

George was undecided on how he should deal with the situation. Should he cough to interrupt them, or push Peter off her? He decided to mull it over and continued to exercise Patch.

The usual members attended the meeting that evening. Everyone turned up at their usual times and in the same order. George noticed Peter had more of a spring in his step; realised he had done for a while and now he knew the reason.

John looked at George as he knelt to pray. Noticed he appeared distant and did not seem interested, like he had something more important on his mind.

George stopped chanting, looked across at Peter and stared at him as though he were in a trance. The mood was tense; so much so, the atmosphere could have been cut with a knife.

John had become one of George's closest friends. They had been through similar life experiences and had both joined the local pub's darts team. He knew Peter and George went back a long way, so he decided not to say anything. Whatever had happened between the two of them, he thought it best he kept out of it.

Peter left the meeting without saying a word and made his way, along the path, towards the bridge.

Intrigued, George watched him.

Elizabeth waited on the bridge. Like an excited little girl, she jumped up and down when she saw Peter and stretched out her arms to greet him.

George saw their embrace. He turned round and checked to see if John had. But John appeared oblivious as he chatted with Fred.

As George put the statue and the mats back into his holdall, he felt let down by Peter. But he hid his disappointment as he straightened up, put the holdall over his shoulder and put his arm around John's shoulders. 'Come on, mate. Let's go to the pub and throw a few darts.' He led John away in the opposite direction. 'See you tomorrow, Fred.' He put up his hand to wave.

Fred looked around. He realised Peter had already left and he was there alone. He enjoyed the meetings, which got him out of the flat, and met people at his shop, which kept him occupied during the day, but the nights were long and lonely. He made his way home.

*

As Elizabeth and Peter sat beside the river, he slipped his hand inside her blouse and spelt *I love you* across her back with his fingertip.

His words tickled her skin; made her wiggle and giggle. She had butterflies in her stomach and felt lightheaded. She continued to giggle as she whispered those same three words back to him.

He cupped her chin in his hand and lifted her face so he could look into her eyes. 'Pardon?' He smiled.

She tittered. 'I said, I love you.'

They laid in each other's arms with their eyes closed.

A moment later, she sat up and looked at him. 'Peter?'

He opened one eye and then the other. His vision was blurred as he looked up at her. 'Yes, Elizabeth?'

'Could you sit up, please? I need to tell you something.' She gestured for him to hurry.

He sat up and with his fingertips, he brushed her hair away from her face and frowned. 'What's wrong? Why do you look so serious?'

She held his hand and bit into her bottom lip. How would he take the news? She cleared her throat with a cough and took a deep breath. 'I'm pregnant. We're going to have a baby.'

Unsure if he had heard correctly, he wiggled his finger inside his ear and said, 'Say that again.'

'I'm –'

But he did not give her time to finish, threw his arms around her and then held her at arm's length. He nodded as he tried to take in the news. 'Oh, my goodness. I'm going to be a dad.' He got to his feet, got down on one knee and said, 'Elizabeth Buckley, will you marry me?'

'Er.' She tittered and tapped her index finger on her chin as she pretended to contemplate his proposal. 'Yes, of course, I'll marry you, but I'll need a big diamond ring.'

Still down on one knee and with a twinkle in his eye, he continued to look at her. 'I love you, Mrs Elizabeth Hurst.'

She liked the sound of those words and tittered again. 'I love you too, Mr Peter Hurst.' She had found the man she wanted to spend the rest of her life with.

*

John and George called in at George's house to drop off the holdall before they went on to their local pub to have a game of darts.

At the pub, George bought the first drinks. They put their pints on a side table and George got his darts from his pocket. 'We need to come up with an idea to recruit more people to our prayer meetings; any ideas, John?'

'I'll put my thinking cap on.' John picked up the board rubber and wiped the previous players chalked scores off the blackboard. 'I've tried to recruit Elizabeth, but she doesn't seem interested.'

'What, too busy?' George closed his left eye, aimed the dart at the dartboard and threw it.

John watched him hit the twenty without a practice shot. 'No, she thinks the meetings are stupid.'

George laughed before he threw his second dart. 'Women, eh!' The dart missed the twenty and landed in the five.

'Where was Hursty rushing off to? His mind seems to be elsewhere lately,' John said. 'He's not got a woman, has he?'

The third dart missed the board and got lodged in the cork backboard. George's temperament changed. 'No idea what he's been up to,' he snapped.

John knew George enjoyed a game of darts, but he had not realised how seriously. 'I thought you guys went back a long way.'

'We do.' George retrieved his darts. As he turned round to look at John, his eyes glared, his jaw clenched, and his nostrils flared. 'But it appears he's only friends when it suits him. He's up to something and he knows I wouldn't approve; hence the secrecy.'

John's shoulders tensed. He decided to drop the subject and finished his pint.

George, who had hoped to throw a few arrows to release tension and take his mind off Peter, decided to call it a night.

They agreed to meet up again the night after, as usual.

John realised George knew something was wrong and had decided to keep the truth from him; however, he decided not to push the matter further and went home.

George was still undecided on what he should do about the Peter and Elizabeth situation. Part of him would have preferred not to have seen them together and to be kept out of it altogether, while the other part wanted to tell John everything and then try to knock some sense into Peter. Going with a friend's woman was a definite no.

Peter, who was first at the meeting the following night, had decided, and nothing or no one would change his mind. It was common knowledge around the neighbourhood that a strange cult practiced in the park, and he no longer wanted to be associated with any part of it. The meetings had been fun while they lasted and a bit of a laugh at first. He had never asked George how he conjured up the small black shadows as he did not want to spoil the illusion.

He noticed George's frown as he approached him and knew something was wrong. 'Look, George, there's something I need to tell you,' he said.

George placed the holdall on the ground beneath the tree, walked towards Peter and stopped in front of him. 'I already know.'

'You do?' Peter gaped. 'I know we go back a long way, it's just, I don't think these meetings are for me anymore.'

George frowned. 'What, you're bailing on me? We've got some new recruits starting tonight, Hursty. You've let me down, mate.' He walked back across to his holdall and started to take out the statue and the prayer mats.

Peter followed and tried to explain, 'Sorry, I've got other things to worry about. We can still meet up and go for a drink, now and again, if you like.'

George was tired of the lies and decided to confront him. He straightened up and looked Peter in the eye. 'What, you mean like John's bird: Elizabeth?' He gauged Peter's facial expression as he waited for him to respond.

Peter's eyes widened. 'What?' He gulped.

'You heard me." George smiled smugly. He shook his head in disgust. 'Don't treat me like a fool as well.'

Peter stepped back and scratched his chin. 'How did you find out about us?'

George looked around to check no one could hear before he said, 'I saw you both together. You weren't exactly being discreet.'

'Shit!' Peter gulped. 'Did John see us? I didn't want him to find out like that.'

'No, not on that occasion. And it's a bit late to start agonising over John's feelings, isn't it?'

Peter nodded, but he felt relieved the secret was out in the open. 'She's pregnant, George. She's having my kid. I'm so excited. I'm going to be a dad.'

'How exciting for you both. Pleased for you, mate.' George might have appeared to assure Peter, but his thoughts were malicious.

'You need to understand. We didn't mean for any of this to happen. It feels right and like it was meant to be. Now I need to tell John. That's going to be the hard part. Got to be honest with him, though. Elizabeth said she'd try to break the news gently to him.'

George placed his hand on Peter's shoulder. 'He already suspects something's going on, but he doesn't know what, at least I don't think he does. Your news might sound better if it came from me. Do you want me to break the news to him?'

'Would you?' Peter tried to work out if George was being sincere or if it was a joke. 'Would you do that for me? You have no idea how much it'd help. Please try to explain that we didn't mean to hurt him.'

George took his hand from Peter's shoulder and punched him gently on the top of his arm. 'We go back a long way, Hursty. Besides, what are friends for? I'm sure you'd do the same for me, wouldn't you?'

All day, Peter had rehearsed how he would break the news to George about the meetings and the news to John about Elizabeth. He could not believe how easy it had been. He had expected someone to kick off; although, his gut feeling still warned him not to feel right about the situation. 'No hard feelings about the meetings? You understand?'

'Yeah, of course, I understand. Go and be with your good lady. Come back down here tomorrow and I'll let you know how I got on.' George winked and gestured with his head for Peter to get on his way.

'Cheers.' Peter grabbed George, hugged him, and patted his back and then off he went with a spring in his step. He felt like a great burden had been lifted from his shoulders.

George watched Peter as he walked away. His chest rose and fell as he tried to control his breathing; slowly, he inhaled and exhaled. His lips were pursed. His nostrils were flared. His face reddened. Peter had disregarded what George believed in; what they had all worked so hard to achieve. He had mocked it; therefore, it was time to move it up to the next level.

'Not joining us tonight, Hursty?' John said as Peter approached him on the path.

Peter neither answered nor looked at John but did acknowledge him with a little wave as he walked by.

John, who had expected a response, stopped, turned round to look at Peter and watched as he quickened his pace. He shrugged, shook his head, and continued along the path towards George.

George, who had calmed down, was setting everything up ready for the meeting.

'Evening. What's wrong with Hursty?' John sensed an atmosphere and he wanted to know what the problem was. 'He seemed to be in a hurry. Walked straight past me; practically ignored me. Have I said or done something to offend him?'

George straightened up, walked across to John, and gripped his shoulders as he looked him in the eye. 'He's left our meetings.' His face filled with rage again.

'Why?' John knew something serious had happened. He wriggled his shoulders to allow the blood to circulate again.

George snapped out of his trance, shook his head, and released John's shoulders. 'I need to speak to you after the meeting, okay?'

Unsure if he felt nervous or relieved, John said, 'Yes, of course.'

A couple of new recruits had joined: young spotty lads who had nothing better to do with their time on a night.

During the meeting, George kept his professionalism while John tried to second-guess what he might want to talk to him about.

As the young lads left, they seemed pleased to be part of something; albeit unusual. Only George and John remained.

'We don't seem to be getting any further than mustering up a few powerless entities, John,' George said as he packed everything away. 'We need a sacrifice and I know just the thing.'

'Sacrifice?' John's eyes widened. He had not expected to hear those words.

'Yes, you heard me right. We need a blood sacrifice.'

John froze as he tried to work out if his surroundings were real or if he was about to wake up in his bed. 'What, you mean like a cat or a dog?'

George laughed. 'No, I mean a human and I know just the individual.' He smiled as he looked at John.

The hairs on the back of John's neck stood on end. 'Not me, please!'

George tittered and shook his head. 'No. Peter Hurst.'

'Are you being serious or are you trying to scare the crap out of me? Because I can tell you, if you are, you're succeeding.' John laughed nervously.

George leant forward, closer to John. 'He's got more important things to be getting on with, so he doesn't want any part of our meetings,' he said.

'So, let me get this straight.' John tilted his head to one side slightly. 'You want to sacrifice him, kill him, because he doesn't want to come to the meetings any more. Do you know how bonkers that sounds?'

George nodded. 'Yes, that's right. He said he's going to come down to the meeting, one last time, tomorrow.'

'So, with a bit of luck, we can change his mind rather than sacrifice him?' John nodded; hopeful George would agree.

'Yes, that's the general idea.' George smirked. He knew in the next twenty-four hours, John would see things from his perspective, just as soon as he found out the truth.

The following day, George rang the two new recruits to let them know the meeting had been cancelled for that evening. He would let them know when the next one would be.

John felt reluctant to go to the meeting. He knew there would be a confrontation but what might happen to him if he did not go?

The following evening George and John arrived early. They sat on the bench and waited for Peter.

Peter arrived a little later.

George got the statue out of his holdall and placed it beneath the sycamore. He left the prayer mats in the holdall.

John still did not understand what all the fuss was about. 'Are you okay, Hursty?'

'I'm okay, John,' Peter said quietly. 'More importantly, how are you? You seem to have taken the news better than I thought you would. I –'

'Right, guys, here's a beer each.' George passed them both a bottle and switched them at the last second. 'Get your laughing gear round these.'

They each took a swig from their bottle.

Not long after, Peter started to feel light-headed. His arms numbed. Unable to move or speak, his legs crumpled, and he fell to the ground beneath the tree. He frothed at the mouth. His eyes rolled to show only the whites.

George had slipped Peter a *Mickey Finn*.

Unable to understand what George had done, John watched in horror. None of it made any sense. He poured what was left of his beer on to the ground, dropped the bottle and grabbed George's arm. 'What the hell are you doing? What's going on? And what was Hursty talking about? He's talking to me like I'm the one who's going to be mincemeat.' He felt his chest tighten and his stomach churn. 'I want answers and I want them now.'

George pulled John's hand away from his arm. 'I hope you're ready for what I'm about to tell you.' His eyes looked different somehow: glassy, like he saw something beyond John's face. 'Not only does Hursty want to leave us but he's going to do it with Elizabeth.'

'Elizabeth?' John frowned and placed his hand over his heart. 'My Elizabeth?'

George nodded. He looked down at Peter and spat a dollop of phlegm on to his face. 'Yes, and if that's not bad enough, she's expecting his baby as well.'

John said nothing. He looked at George and Peter in turn. His head spun as he tried to take in what George had said. *Who are these men? What have I got myself involved in? Is George telling me the truth? Peter would never do that to me.* He shook his head. *She told me the meetings were foolish, but she has been more distant with me lately and made-up stupid excuses for us not to be together.* He concluded Peter had set out to take her from him as he snapped back to reality.

George grabbed Peter by his arms, dragged and then propped him against the tree, beneath the pentangle, beside the statue. He got a length of rope from out of his holdall and wound it around Peter and the tree.

John lunged, knelt in front of Peter, and punched him on his nose.

Tears of pain and regret poured from Peter's eyes and streamed down his face. Blood oozed from both nostrils. He had heard, smelt, and sensed everything before it happened but was powerless to stop any of it.

George took a flick knife from out of his holdall, passed it to John and nodded his head.

As though John had been able to read George's mind, he knew what had to be done. He stabbed Peter in his chest; felt the softness of his heart. He pulled the knife out and counted aloud as he stabbed him, repeatedly.

Bright red frothy blood pulsated and flowed down Peter towards the ground. The tree's roots absorbed the blood and started to quiver. As the pentangle appeared to fill with blood, the tree took on a life of its own.

Out of control, John's anger engulfed him.

George grabbed John's arm to stop him; tried to divert his attention as he pointed at the statue.

Alongside the usual small black shadows hovered a larger black shadow. It looked down at them and Peter's lifeless body.

George fell to his knees and bowed down to the black shadow; idolised it as though it were a God; offered to surrender his soul.

However, it did not acknowledge him.

He looked up at it and watched as it disappeared. He got to his feet and looked down at the statue. He felt cheated; the black shadow had not given him chance to prove his worth.

John got to his feet, looked down at Peter's body and then at the knife which was still in his possession. He opened his hand. The knife fell to the ground. There were sores across his palm where he had gripped the knife. He had blacked out and could not remember what had happened during the last few minutes.

The realisation he had just murdered another human hit him. He gasped for breath; his chest tightened; his heart rate quickened. He rushed behind the tree and grabbed its trunk with one hand while he held his stomach with the other. He lurched forward and vomited twice. He tried to lift his head but retched again. He caught his breath, wiped away any residual vomit from his lips with the back of his hand and wiped it down his trousers.

George used the same bloodied knife to cut Peter free of the tree. No one saw as they dragged his corpse into a bush.

'I was so angry, George.' John looked down at his bloodied hands. 'I must have hit out before I realised what I was doing. I've never killed anyone before. You've got to believe me.'

George led John down to the river to wash his hands.

John wept and his body shook.

'Don't worry, we'll find somewhere to bury him.' George placed his hand on John's shoulder and looked across at the statue. He felt more disappointed about the black shadow than he did about Peter's death. He had researched the occult for years and was unsure what would happen. He wished the gateway to hell had appeared. 'We can't do it down here, though. We'll be seen and the animals will probably dig him up.'

John knew he could trust George. He was, after all, an accessory to Peter's murder. 'Okay.'

All too conveniently, George came up with a solution. 'What about your back garden?' He had obviously given the idea some serious thought.

'Okay.' John, who felt confused and vulnerable, would have gone along with anything George had suggested.

'Have you got a wheelbarrow and something to cover his body with?' George said. Any outsider might have found it hard to believe that the corpse had been his long-time friend.

John nodded. 'I should have.'

They headed back towards the bush.

'Fetch them while I stay here with the body,' George said. He looked left and then right as though he stood guard.

By the time John returned, darkness had fallen. The task had taken longer than expected. He had needed to change out of his bloodied clothes and find oil for his squeaky wheelbarrow as he had not wanted to draw any unnecessary attention. 'Everything okay?' he said as he looked around the ground for any signs of evidence.

'Yes. You took a long time. Did anyone see you?' George had put the statue back into his holdall and had covered the patch of blood beneath the tree with soil; any passer-by might have assumed a scavenging animal had made the mess.

'Well, yes, but no one questioned or bothered me.' John noticed sweat beads on George's brow. He wondered if something had happened while he had been gone.

George checked around before he grabbed Peter's wrists and dragged him from the bush. 'We're going to have to be quick.'

John grabbed Peter's ankles.

George continued, 'After three. One. Two. Three, lift.' He gasped. 'Jesus, he weighs a ton.' They threw the corpse into the wheelbarrow as though he were a dead animal. They turned him on to his side, tried to curl him into a ball, threw an old wool blanket over him and made sure he was covered. George uprooted a few plants and bushes and balanced them on top. If anyone spotted them, they would presume they had simply pilfered a few plants from the park.

The walk to John's was not far. They were sure no one had seen them. The wheelbarrow struggled but made the distance.

With no light, except from the moon and nearby streetlights, they took it in turns to dig a hole in John's back garden. Neither of them said a word as they lowered the corpse into the grave and filled it over with soil.

George slept on John's living room floor that night. He woke early the next morning and as he left, he closed the front door, gently, behind him.

John, who had not slept a wink, heard George as he left. All night he had waited for Peter to walk into his bedroom or for the police to knock on his front door. Of course, neither had happened, which seemed to disturb him more.

George needed to get cleaned-up before he went to work. He made his way home via the park. As he made his way towards the sycamore, it occurred to him that he would never see Peter again.

He put his holdall on the ground, beside the soil which covered Peter's blood, and took a deep breath. He followed the trail of flattened grass and looked inside the bush where they had temporarily hidden Peter's corpse. There was a brown wallet on the ground. He reached inside, picked it up and when he opened it, he discovered it was Peter's. Inside were a couple of bank cards and ten- and twenty-pound notes. He took the notes out, put them into his pocket and tossed the wallet, along with the cards, into the river.

Someone or something was behind him. He could sense their anger. The hairs on the back of his neck and on his arms stood on end. He did not dare to turn round to check.

The black shadow hovered. It grew taller and wider until it leant forward and wrapped itself around him.

Together, they soared and stopped beneath a thick branch of the sycamore. A rope swing coiled around his neck. The rope tightened. His eyes widened as he started to choke.

The black shadow, who had released him, looked up and watched from beneath the tree.

George tried to loosen the rope, but it gripped his throat like a vice. As he swung his body and kicked his legs to weaken the branch, a python slithered along that same branch towards him. He looked up when he heard a hissing sound. It stuck out its forked tongue and stared at him through piercing dark eyes. When he put up his hands to protect his face, his neck snapped, and his body flinched. Nearby birds took flight. The snake vanished along with the black shadow and the holdall.

His body hung for an hour before a young lady, who had been out for a morning jog, discovered him.

*

Fred, who had been ill for several days, had taken to his bed with a bout of flu. He had heard through the grapevine of George's suicide, but his thoughts were with his son. Concerned about Peter's whereabouts, he had tried several times, every day, to contact him.

A few days later, Peter appeared when Fred was at work in his shop. He heard his son call out to him from the stockroom.

'Dad!'

Fred looked up from his newspaper and smiled. 'Peter?' He made his way into the stockroom and looked around for him. 'Peter?' He frowned. There was no sign of him.

'Dad, I'm so sorry. I never got chance to say goodbye.'

'Goodbye? What do you mean? And why can't I see you?' He looked around again as though his eyes deceived him.

'Please look out for Elizabeth. She's carrying your grandchild.'

'What's going on, Peter? George was found hanging from a tree in Beechwood.' He could smell Peter's aftershave and knew he was close by. 'I'm scared.'

'Please, don't be scared. Everything'll be fine. I promise. I love you, Dad.'

Fred knew Peter was gone; he sensed an emptiness around him. 'I love you too, Son.' He placed his hand on his chest, over his heart.

*

Elizabeth had not heard from Peter for days. She had known something was wrong. He never would have stood her up intentionally.

One evening, she went out for dinner with John to the local Indian restaurant. While they ate their starters, she held back tears as he explained how Peter would not be around anymore. He had seen her eyes well up but chose to ignore it. 'Would you like to move in with me, Elizabeth?'

That was the last question she had expected to hear. She did not answer straight away. An uncomfortable silence followed. She had planned to tell John about

Peter and her; instead, she had to make a quick decision for the sake of her baby. 'Okay, John.' She smiled. 'Thank you. I'd like to move in with you.' She saved her tears for later. Her heart was broken, and it would take a long time to heal.

Chapter Twelve

Happy Ever After

Lisa needed time to herself. She smiled as she made her way along the corridor towards the exit. As she walked past sad and happy faces, she wondered briefly what other people's worries were. Her own news had made her feel like she could take on the world. She was delighted John was not her real father and a man named Peter was, a man she knew nothing about or had heard of until that day.

Grandma, who had stretched her legs, was on her way back to the ward when she met Lisa. Her varicose veins, which could be seen through her tan stockings, and her obvious frailness did not stop her. She stood beside Lisa, leant back, and rubbed her lower back. 'Are you okay, my dear?' She pursed her lips and then winced.

Lisa waited until grandma had straightened up. 'That news was a bit of a surprise, but if I'm being honest, I've had a suspicion something wasn't right since I can remember. I've always known I was different. A lot of what's happened makes sense now and it's all clicked into place.' She put her hand on grandma's arm. 'I'm made of strong stuff you know.' She paused. 'Anyway, are you okay, Grandma?'

Grandma chuckled and then tried to divert any attention away from herself with an attempt at humour, 'Just a bit of old age and a lot of poverty, my dear.' She changed the subject. 'Are you leaving us already?'

'I am, yes.' Lisa hugged grandma. Grandma's familiar smell triggered memories of the cuddles they used to have. 'It was lovely to see you. A shame it wasn't under better circumstances. I'm sure I'll see you again, soon, though. I've got a few jobs I need to do, and I'm going to go and visit a few of my old haunts.'

'Take care of yourself, Lisa. Thanks for ringing me and your grandad to confirm what we'd always suspected about John.' She grabbed Lisa's hand, kissed the back of it and then squeezed it gently. She was in no hurry to let go. 'Are you sure you're, okay? You look a little peaky.'

'Honestly, Grandma, I'll be fine. I'm a bit nauseous. I'm sure it'll pass. It's probably something I ate at breakfast.' She smiled and then kissed the back of grandma's hand. 'Let's not leave it as long next time, though.'

'I always used to have a bit of milk and a plain biscuit when I felt nauseous.' Grandma winked. 'Anyway, bye, love; keep in touch; don't be a stranger.'

As Lisa continued towards the exit, she stopped and looked over her shoulder.

Grandma waved.

Lisa waved, smiled, and then continued.

There was a pharmacy around the corner from the hospital. As she made her way back towards the car, she stopped and looked through the window; undecided if to go inside. Her late period might have been stress related and the sickness could have been down to overindulgence at breakfast or a change in the water.

She decided to leave the pregnancy test kit and headed towards her car.

By the time she got back to the bed and breakfast her nausea had passed; however, she felt tired. A rest was all she needed before she ventured out again. She turned on the radio, sat on the edge of the bed and looked at her reflection in the mirror. She slowly turned her head to the left and then to the right while she kept her eyes on her reflection. It was obvious, now she knew, she looked nothing like John. She imagined what Peter might have looked like.

As she laid down on top of the duvet, she hoped Elizabeth would find a photograph of him and that it would be small enough to carry around in her purse. Her head sank into the pillow, and she dozed to the sounds of an eighties band.

She was woken by her neighbours as their headboard thumped against the wall. She shook her head and tittered; surely the man had not fallen for the woman's fake orgasmic screeches. She got up and made her way into the bathroom.

As she ran a bubble bath, she left the bathroom door ajar. Out of the corner of her eye, she noticed a bright flashing light. She turned her head to check where it came from. It was in the bedroom.

She turned off the hot water tap and cautiously made her way back into the bedroom.

The television picture flickered. Had she accidently leant on the remote when she was laid on the bed? She tried to find the remote: looked under the duvet and pillows, and on the floor around the bed. She found it beside the television and noticed the radio had been turned off. She reached for the remote to turn off the television but stopped when the scene on the screen looked familiar. The setting was inside the old family home.

Intrigued, she sat on the edge of the bed and started to watch John, who was sat in his usual chair, with his feet rested on the coffee table, as he watched the television. The big toe of his left foot poked all the way through a hole in his sock. The living room appeared smoggy. His ashtray overflowed. A lit cigarette stub, which was on top of the mound, had started to burn through another filter.

He lit another cigarette and started to cough as he drew on it. His face reddened and his temporal veins bulged. A dollop of phlegm flew from his mouth and landed on the carpet at the other side of the room.

Five small black shadows drifted in through the kitchen door. They hovered behind him for a moment until the larger black shadow had joined them.

It appeared and hovered in front of him to obscure his line of sight.

He leant sideways, took a drag of his cigarette, and continued to watch the television.

It stayed still for a moment longer until the television and every other electrical device inside the house turned off, simultaneously.

He stood up and looked at it.

It drifted out of the living room, through the kitchen and out through the back door.

Lisa reached behind her, grabbed a pillow, hugged it, and bit her thumbnail as she continued to watch the screen.

John followed the black shadow. He stopped by the back door and grabbed the handle.

It popped its head back through the door and waited until it had heard him gulp.

He pulled the handle down and stepped outside.

As it hovered over the lawn where Peter was buried, it waited for his reaction.

His eyes widened and a sweat bead rolled down his temple. 'What the ... Hursty?'

The scenery on the screen changed to Beechwood Park. A younger John spoke with a man she did not recognise. There was no longer any sound; like an old silent movie where the actors mimed.

As she leant forward and moved closer to the screen, she felt she should know the man who walked along the path towards them. It was not until he got closer, she realised who he might be. Was he her real father? He could have been her twin. She reached out to the screen and said, 'Dad?'

Peter turned his head, looked her in the eye and smiled.

She gasped and flinched back.

The man, who had stood beside a young John, got three bottles of beer from out of his holdall. He opened them with a bottle opener, popped a couple of pills into one of them and passed that bottle to Peter.

'No,' she screamed at the screen.

Peter did not turn his head.

Her heart sank as she watched him gulp from the bottle. Her chin quivered as she sobbed. Through her tears, she watched him fall to the ground. She realised she had witnessed her father's murder. A sequence of events followed, up to the burial of his corpse.

There had never been any bank robbery. Elizabeth was unaware of the truth.

Lisa picked up the telephone and rang John. She wanted to tell him that she knew the truth and what she thought of him. But he did not answer. She slammed the telephone down, grabbed a tissue and wept some more.

The television switched itself off and the radio station resumed.

*

John had heard the telephone ring, but it rang off as he rushed back inside the house. He locked the door behind him as he believed it would keep Peter out.

Although he wanted to run, he remained calm and made his way upstairs.

As he rummaged through Elizabeth's wardrobe, he found an old shoe box hidden at the back underneath a pile of blankets. He threw the blankets on the floor and tipped the box's contents out, over the bed. Handmade greeting cards, which had been given to her by her girls, laid alongside locks of hair, baby shoes and pieces of ribbon; all sentimental items which held a special place in her heart.

An address book fell out of the box and a photograph of Peter, which had been inside, fell out, face up. The photograph appeared to stare at John as he picked it up. 'You're dead, Hursty. You've been dead for years. Now go away.' As he tore it into little pieces, he sensed he was no longer alone.

Lisa's real father; her guardian angel; the black shadow hovered in the doorway. It moved and hovered beside John.

John's chest tightened and he struggled to breathe. 'You deserved to die.' He spluttered and coughed as he tried to move away but he was backed against a wall.

It gripped him by his neck and lifted him off the floor.

His face reddened and he started to choke. He closed his bloodshot eyes.

It released him.

He fell to the floor and rubbed his neck.

It ascended and hovered above him.

He looked up, tried to act brave but he knew his days were probably numbered. 'Why now after all these years? What took you so long, Peter Hurst?'

It continued to hover before it moved closer and then disappeared.

The television in the living room turned back on. The local news was on. All the other electrical equipment, throughout the house, turned on, one after the other.

He felt relieved as he believed the situation to be over. Confident that if Peter had wanted revenge, he would have finished him a long time ago.

A sensation of weightlessness overcame him as his feet left the floor again. He flew at speed and caused the ceiling light shade to sway. As he hit the bedroom wall at the other side of the room, his back cracked, and he fell to the floor. He screamed in agony and tears rolled down his face. 'Did you seriously think I wouldn't find out about you? That I wouldn't do a bit of research on you. I knew you'd been sniffing round my Elizabeth,' he lied. His pain worsened. He grimaced. His breathing grew louder. He laid on the floor, unable to move. 'Is that all you've got for me?' he screamed.

A bedside table lamp crashed to the floor. The bulb broke and untwisted before it flew across the room and slashed his cheek.

It appeared again and hovered above him. 'I could have made Elizabeth so happy,' it said. 'Much happier than your pathetic effort. The only woman I ever loved, and you took me away from her. You messed up. Now it is my turn to look after her and Lisa but not before I give you what I should have given you a long time ago.' Again, it disappeared and all around felt calmer.

He breathed another sigh of relief. Still unable to move, he scanned the room to make sure he was alone. The telephone was not within reach. He would have to wait until someone came to visit before he could be moved. The pain became too much, and he closed his eyes to sleep.

Almost immediately, he opened his eyes to the sound of laughter.

Once again, the black shadow hovered above him. It descended and reached down into his chest cavity while its relentless laughter continued.

He flapped his arms around and made it distort but was not able to grab it or push it away.

It encased his heart within its hand and squeezed until its hand became a fist and his heart no longer beat.

Lisa and Susan found his body later that day when they went round to collect some of Elizabeth's belongings.

The coroner's report said he had died from a heart attack. He would have died instantly and not felt any pain.

Susan was the only one who cried at his funeral, which was a quiet, close family affair; none of his friends attended.

The months flew by. Elizabeth spent several weeks in Spain with her parents. The family home was put on the market and sold. She boxed up her belongings ready to move in with Lisa.

Lisa decided to keep the whereabouts of Peter's grave a secret.

The day of the move arrived. Two men had the house emptied into a removal van in no time. Most of the furniture and ornaments were headed for the local charity shop. They left long before Lisa picked Elizabeth up in her car.

Elizabeth stood outside the front door. The house keys dangled from her hand ready to drop off at the estate agents.

Lisa wound down the car window. 'You ready, Mum?' she shouted through the trees.

Elizabeth made her way towards her with a huge grin on her face.

Lisa jumped out of the car and hugged her. 'Well, how do you feel, Mum? You ready for your new adventure?'

'I am. I said my goodbyes to Susan and her family yesterday. They said they'll try and visit as much as they can.' Elizabeth looked over Lisa's shoulder into the back seat of the car. 'Well, are you going to introduce me to the new man in your life?'

Lisa opened the back door.

When Elizabeth poked her head inside the car, she was greeted with a cheeky smile. 'Hello, sweetheart,' she said.

Lisa reached inside, unbuckled his safety seat, and then passed the tiny bundle of joy to Elizabeth. 'Grandma Elizabeth, meet your grandson.'

Elizabeth cradled him and stroked his cheeks with her fingers. 'He's beautiful. I love him already. Have you thought of a name for him, yet?'

'Yes, I have.' Lisa put her arm around Elizabeth's shoulders. 'I know you're going to love it.' She smiled. 'I'm going to call him Peter.'

Elizabeth's chin quivered and her eyes welled up. 'Oh, how lovely, your dad would've been so proud.'

Baby Peter had fallen asleep in his grandma's arms. She carefully put him back into his seat and fastened him in before she sat beside Lisa on the passenger seat.

They were on their way. Neither of them looked back. Lisa knew everything would turn out good as she looked in the rear-view mirror and saw the black shadow watch over Peter as he slept.

Printed in Great Britain
by Amazon